I0529679

# A Wolf's Bargain

*Black Hills Wolves Book 59*

By
## TL Reeve

This book is a work of fiction. Names, characters, places, and incidents are the products of the author's imagination or used fictitiously. Any resemblance to actual events, locales or persons, living or dead, is entirely coincidental.

Published by
Decadent Publishing Company, LLC

Look for us online at:
www.decadentpublishing.com

Dear Readers,

Thank you for picking up a copy of A Wolf's Bargain. I loved writing Chris and Lily's story. They were a handful the moment I wrote them into Winter Magic, and they continued to be one throughout A Wolf's Contract and A Wolf's Deception. And, boy, in this story does she go down fighting tooth and claw.

There is a twist to this story though. What you'll have to read. And, there is some sadness as well. Things happen for a reason and I promise you, it will become clear in future books.

I hope you enjoy *A Wolf's Bargain*.

**TL**
www.tlreeves.com
www.facebook.com/tl.reeve2014

# Dedication

To you, the readers, thank you.

# Chapter One

"How's Lily been?" Chris waited at the side of the round pen for Kalum to push the cattle into position. "Haven't seen her in town for a while."

The crisp morning air reminded him it had almost been a year since he'd kissed Lily. A year since he'd held her in his arms. They'd always had a bond between them. However, it took kissing her for him to put it all together. The realization she belonged to him had swept through him like an out-of-control freight train. And, ever since then, he'd battled his domineering wolf, who demanded he take what was rightfully his.

"When are you going to suck it up and talk to her?" Kalum closed the chute on the first heifer, allowing him to administer a booster for her vaccinations.

"Believe me, I've tried." He'd put himself in her way several times, to broach the subject of their mating, but she'd have none of it.

When he left a little over ten years ago, Chris had never envisioned returning. But the wide open spaces of Wyoming called to him and his wolf. He had aspirations of owning his own veterinarian clinic out on forty acres. Animals big or small would be welcome there. The only thing missing? Lily.

"Really?" Kal cocked a brow.

"Yeah. I have." He patted the cow on the rear after releasing her. "She's being stubborn. Seems like it runs in the family."

He yearned for the little curly-haired, slate-blue eyed girl. She'd climbed under his skin and become irritating, in the best of ways. A scratch he couldn't sate. He *had* to be in her presence.

"She's got you whipped, and you haven't even mated her yet." His friend laughed.

Chris flipped him off. "Don't tell me you're not wrapped around Fawn's little finger."

His chest puffed up. "Damn straight I am. She knows I'll do anything for her whenever she needs it. It's my duty and my pleasure."

"Then, why are you giving me shit?"

"Let me give you a piece of advice. Don't give her too much space. The more you do, the more she'll take advantage."

He had an inkling. "I won't push her, either, though. I want a willing mate. Not some messed-up husk of a mate."

Magnum had been a nasty bastard—insane beyond comprehension and mate deprived. He couldn't imagine putting someone into a horrible headspace, especially if it was Lily. Just the thought of it turned his stomach and pissed his wolf off.

Kal nodded. "I think too much has happened in the last six months."

He'd figured as much. With their brother,

Graham, spending time with Elle and her human companion, Kizzy, Lily had been left to her own devices. She had fallen into the role her mother left behind of caring for her siblings, but the time had come for her to start her own life.

"True. At least she has Gabby to talk to." Sometimes. Even she had been spending more and more time at home with Kru. As soon as he knew his mate carried his pups, Kru had turned into an overprotective pit bull. He didn't blame the guy. She was carrying twins, after all.

His best friend shook his head. "I thought she had it all under control. I believe she's feeling...left out."

He sighed, glancing down at his boots. "Well, she's not. I'm right here."

Though he tried to hide his Dominant side and the urges he'd sated for years while in Wyoming, she'd never seemed interested in him. Several times, he'd thought about throwing caution to the wind—even though it went against his need to protect her psyche—and take her to the dungeon owned by Ogre and Kennedy Laurie, Patch Williams's mate. As a member, Chris believed it would be the perfect place for him to explore his soon-to-be mating with Lily. Would she accept Hippogriff—the name he used while at the club? If she accepted the man he was, could she come to the dungeon with him and explore the many playrooms? Perhaps indulge him in a public scene or three? No, he couldn't allow himself to wonder about these things. Until he knew for sure how she'd react to his brand of pleasure, he'd keep it to himself.

"Looks like you have your work cut out for you."

Kal smacked him on the back. "You don't need my permission to do this. But, I'm giving it to you anyway. It's past time she grows up. Settles down."

No, he didn't need Kal's permission, but he understood why his friend gave it to him. Like Lily taking on her mother's role, he'd taken on their father's. As the protector of their family, Kalum made damn sure they all stayed safe and had someone to turn to when they needed him most. In a way, he was glad Lily had her brothers. Because of them, she'd become a strong-willed, woman who drove him nuts—not like he minded the last part one bit.

"Didn't you just have this conversation with Graham?" All of the rumors about Elle's death had turned out to be speculation. Her parents, along with Ryker's help, had sent her away to North Carolina where she met Kizzy, her best friend. Surprised the shit out of all of them. Hell, he'd mourned her as well. To see her the first time after so many years had left him speechless and relieved. *One more story of survival to add to the many.*

Kal pushed his hat up. "'Spose I did. Saw how good it turned out."

Chris laughed. "Yep. Your brother has his hands full, not only with his mate, but with her friend, too."

"Yes, he does." He turned away from the round pen and started for the house. Smoke poured from the chimney. Over the last couple of weeks, the weather had taken a decided downward turn, and, a few days ago, they'd gotten their first dusting of snow. A short-lived reminder of what was to come. "I'm sure Lily will have lunch ready. Seems the girls are always hungry lately."

He bet. "Sure, sounds great."

The last few months changed the Truesdale family. After the tumultuous start of the year with the murders then a crazed man hell-bent on killing Gabby, Kru's mate, it seemed no matter how bad it got, the hills were always evolving. Thankfully, though, things had started slowing down. Time to show his mate what they could have if only she allowed him to guide her.

"Have you given much thought on how you'll make this work?" He glanced at his friend as they got into the truck.

"No...well, technically, yes, but I'm not sure it will. She's not been receptive to any of the advances I've made so far. It might take a while to figure out a new plan of attack." Talking about Lily always got him in a snit. He had so much planned for them. Yet, every time he saw an opportunity to pounce, she rebuffed him, sending him on to the next idea.

"Well, you've got plenty of time."

He hoped. "She's got me antsy." A feeling he hated with a passion. He'd felt the same thing only days before he made his escape. He loved his parents dearly and knew nothing would make them leave the hills, which ratcheted up his anxiety about leaving to begin with.

"She's got all of us in knots." His friend laughed. "I think it's because she's the youngest."

"You mean the baby."

"Don't let her hear you say that."

He shrugged. Better not to deny the truth than avoid it. When they pulled up to the ranch house, Jordan, Tinks's son, stood near the fence, petting one of the cows, while Kip, Kalum's border collie, stood sentinel over the ten-year-old boy.

"How's he doing?" He'd learned about the boy after coming home. The poor kid. No one knew who his parents were. Tinks and Bobbi, her sister, found him wrapped in swaddling next to the creek. When no one came to claim the boy as their kin, she became his mother.

"The kid is a natural with animals."

Lily had offered to watch over the boy while Tinks worked in town. Her artwork had become such a hot commodity she'd begun the arduous task of renovating one of the derelict storefronts for a gallery of sorts. The Burrows men were doing all the heavy-duty work of tearing down walls and laying drywall while she designed the layout and what would be painted on the walls. The long hours took her away from the boy, but he seemed quite content to be on the ranch. Kids, wolves more specifically, needed to socialize.

"The Burrows clan has a couple of kids. Jessie, she's a mite of a thing, a little young. I bet they'd be good friends. Why don't you set up a play date or whatever the hell they're called nowadays?"

Kalum gave him a skeptical look. "Playdates?"

"Hey, you're the one prepping for this shit. I'm still trying to get my mate to pay me five minutes of attention." He laughed.

"I'll talk to Lily and Tinks about it." Kal grunted. "I can't believe I'm having this conversation with you and my pup isn't even here yet." He opened the truck door. "Who'd have thought all those years ago when we spent summers bailing hay, we'd one day become domesticated?"

Chris barked out a laugh. "Speak for yourself."

They got out of Kalum's truck then started for

the house. "Hey, kid," Chris called out. "I bet Lily has made something great for lunch. You'd better get cleaned up or else you'll get scraps."

The kid frowned then ran for the house. *Smooth move.* He knew everyone, especially Tinks, had struggled for a long time to make ends meet—hell, the whole pack had. "Shit."

Kal gave his shoulder a squeeze. "Want help getting your foot out of your mouth?"

"I have a feeling I'm going to need it." He frowned.

Stepping inside the mudroom, he removed his vest, hung it up then discarded his boots. As soon as he entered the kitchen, he'd get an earful from the womenfolk.

"What's for lunch?" Kal passed him and crossed to his mate.

"Scraps," Lily replied. Her curly brown hair had been pulled up into a messy bun, allowing some of the wavy locks to frame her heart-shaped face. Her full, bow lips were pulled in a thin line as she glared at him.

His dick thickened at the challenge held in those slate-blue eyes.

*Shit.* He sauntered into the room. "Sorry. I should have chosen my words better." He glanced at Jordan whose plate had been piled high with lunch fixings. The kid chewed and swallowed faster than a jackrabbit being chased by a coyote.

Lily gave him a flippant look then went to the stove. *Great, you've really gone and done it.* Chris took a seat next to Jordan and stilled the hand-to-mouth gorge fest going on. "Easy, kid. I used the wrong words. No one is going to take anything from you."

"Don't let Chris give you a hard time, either. You'd think he was raised by a pack of wolves or something." Kal nuzzled his mate's neck, smiling at her giggle before he took the plate Lily handed him. "Thanks, little bit."

The boy looked up at him, cheeks bloated, looking more like a chipmunk than a wolf. He gave a curt nod then finished eating what he'd shoveled into his mouth. "Okay."

Without a word, Lily placed a dish in front of Chris. He frowned at the meager fixings. A few slices of fried potatoes, the smallest sliver of steak, and a handful of peas. However, he didn't bitch about it. He'd caused the mess. He'd deal with it. "Thank you, Lily."

She rolled her eyes at him, and he fisted his hands under the table. The wild, dismissive streak running through her called to his wolf. The part of him demanding her submission, no matter what it took.

He ate in silence, finishing before the others got their lunch. "I'll see you later, Kalum. Call me if you need anything." Chris ruffled Jordan's hair then stood.

"Are you sure you have to go?" Fawn rubbed her belly.

He nodded. "I have an appointment in Rapid City."

She frowned. "Come back for dinner, then."

*Little minx.* Chris gave her a knowing look. "I'll see what I can do." He stepped over to the stove where Lily stood. "Thanks for lunch." He leaned in and kissed her temple. "I'm sorry."

Her slate-blue eyes dilated with need. "Whatever." Her sassy tone belied her demeanor.

"Soon, she-wolf," he growled low.

He hated leaving her. Hated the fact he couldn't stay and teach her a lesson. Couldn't take her over his knee and spank her ass. Tie her up and tease her ruthlessly until she begged him for relief. As he entered the mudroom, he grabbed his vest then put his boots back on. With a last backward glance, he walked out of the house and headed toward his truck.

Damn it, he could kick his own ass right now. What the hell had he been thinking? *You weren't. That's the problem.* He climbed into his truck and glanced at the house. So much for being smooth. About the best thing happening in his favor was Kalum's go-ahead.

He had to come up with the perfect plan. Something Lily couldn't say no to. *Well, you have time, asshole. Especially after today.*

# Chapter Two

Lily curled her lip. Why the hell had she kissed him at the Winter Solstice festivities? From the moment Chris had pointed toward the mistletoe then pressed his lips to hers, she couldn't stop thinking about him. Or, maybe, it was because he always seemed to be right in her way. She smacked the spatula against the pan a little too hard and winced. The whole time Chris ate his lunch, she kept her back to him, hoping to quell the need to rub up against him.

Over the last several months, he'd inserted himself more and more into her life. After the trip to Hill City when she, Fawn, Gabby, and Alicia had been kidnapped by a biker named Player, Chris had been on her ass. Of course, it had made her feel a little more in control, though she'd never say as much to him. The idea of telling him anything made her pulse race. Not in anger, but with desire. She craved him more than she'd ever wanted anyone. More than she'd admit.

"You know"—Kal took his seat beside Fawn—"he

didn't mean any harm. You should cut him some slack."

"You would stick up for him." She turned and pointed the cooking utensil at him.

"No, I'm not sticking up for him. I'm saying it because you were fucking rude to him." It took an awful lot for him to curse. Even when he'd rescued them from Player, he hadn't cussed.

"Well, excuse me. I forgot teasing pack pups is a free pass. I'll remember it when your child is born."

"Lily," Fawn admonished, "you're being mean. I don't like it. In fact, you've been this way for months. Maybe longer."

She winced. Her anger, though on point, was irrational. Chris hadn't meant what he'd said to Jordan, and they'd never let the boy starve, nor would Elle. Still, whatever motherly instinct she had deep down inside of her tripped at the mention of "scraps" if the boy didn't hurry up.

"Whatever," she snapped. "He had no business teasing Jordan." She pointed to the boy who sat happily eating his lunch.

"If you're upset with Chris, talk to the guy. He meant no harm."

He never did. "I realize this. Sometimes, he pushes buttons."

Her mated sister laughed. "Yes, he does. His heart will always be in the right place, and he apologized."

The anger subsided in Lily, and she sighed. "When you're finished, Jordan, why don't you see if Graham will saddle up one of the mares for you to ride?"

His face lit up, and he practically bounced in his

chair. "Really?"

"Yes, really. You've been doing really well. I think"—she glanced at Fawn who nodded—"he'll even take you through the pastureland to see all the cows."

He finished his lunch with gusto then cleaned his plate off and placed it in the sink. He gave Lily a quick hug then Fawn, whose rounded belly he rubbed before he hurried out the door.

"He is a ball of energy." Fawn laughed.

"Yes, he is."

Once she had the dishes done, she joined Fawn in the living room. Gabby would be there shortly to plan their baby showers. She'd learned about the human tradition a few years after they moved away from the hills. Her mother had become quite the PTA parent, which meant invitations of all kinds popping up in their mailbox.

The first couple of times they went, Lily and her mom sat there a little wide-eyed. The games had been somewhat outrageous like guess what's in the diaper, or guess the baby food. Another game required them to slam a bottle of apple juice, and the one with the fastest time won. Then there were the gifts. Fancy baptismal dresses, even for boys. Cute little outfits, blankets, and bottles. Things for the moms. Baby swings and carriers. It blew their minds.

By the third party, they were old hat at it. They didn't feel so out of place. When they finally found their footing, they had a blast. She wanted Fawn and Gabby to have the same experience every one of the moms-to-be they knew had.

"Knock, knock," Gabby called out from the door.

"This house is yours, too." Lily got up to open the door. "You can always come on in."

Gabby laughed. "Well, I wouldn't want to walk in at an inopportune time."

Though she'd stopped dying her hair, the faux-hawk remained. As did her funky clothes. The deep-purple, off-the-shoulder sweater she wore complimented her whimsical-print leggings. The spunky woman had traded her life for Lily, Fawn, Elle, and Alicia's. Lily had been angry and scared leaving her behind when Player had kidnapped them. If she had to do it all over again, she would have taken Drew's punishment for shifting in front of a human—which was a total no-no for the pack. It would have been worth it. Instead, they ran. Instinctively, she knew why Gabby did it. She was protecting the pack and her friends. But, sometimes, loyalty and saving one's life weren't mutually exclusive.

"The men are out poking around, and Jordan is going for a ride. So, we're all alone." Fawn hugged her. "How are you feeling today?"

"Mule kicked." Her friend gave a breathy laugh. "These two are active little buggers." She brushed the side of her belly with her palm. "Kru has already begun disciplining them, in utero. When they get too rambunctious, he presses his nose to my belly and growls softly."

Fawn chuckled. "Leave it to my brother."

"I think he might also enjoy seeing me pregnant." She blushed a little. "Since morning sickness became a thing of the past, he's been amorous."

Lily's gut clenched as envy seeped into her system. "You're positively glowing."

"Thank you." Gabby gave her a shy grin.

"Although I feel bad."

Lily narrowed her eyes. "Why?"

"Here we are, all mated, and you're alone."

She sat back, speechless. What did she say? "I'm okay. It's no big deal."

Fawn sighed. "She's resisting. She knows who her mate is."

"Chris?"

Mortified, Lily crossed her arms. "Does everyone know?"

"The kiss at last year's Solstice celebration was pretty hot." Fawn shrugged. "I guess we all figured you'd end up mated."

"Because of a kiss?" Her insides heated as she remembered the minute their lips had touched. Everything had gone silent. The festivities had disappeared. The idle chatter no longer existed. Chris deepened the kiss. *Mate. Mine.* She shook her head.

"Yes," Fawn answered.

She snorted then shrugged. Grabbing her notepad off the table next to her, Lily changed the subject. "I've been thinking about things to do at your party."

"Deflection." Gabby laughed. "You're good at it."

Lily brushed off the comment. "I really wanted to give each of you a separate day, since your due dates are different, but I thought it would be more fun to have a double celebration, since we're family."

"I have a concern." Gabby's tone turned serious as they got comfortable in the living room. "What about Alicia and Poppa? Not to mention Hombre and Black Jack."

When Gabby came to the hills, her family had followed. They'd settled in Hill City, and whenever she wanted to visit them, she did. But if they wanted to include them, they'd have to have the party outside the pack territory. "Why can't we do it at their home? It's not like we'll go furry while in town." She looked to Fawn for her approval.

"Sure." Fawn smiled. "I don't mind. We'll all be there, and it'll give some of our friends a chance to meet your family. I'll have Kalum let Drew know. I'm sure he won't have a problem with it."

She blew out a breath. "Thank you."

"Of course," Fawn answered. "No way Alicia can miss this. Those are her grandbabies, too."

"Since we have a location, what about—?"

"Sorry I'm late," Elle called out pushing into the house. "Things have been hectic with Brie."

"We just started." Lily grinned. "We have a location set. Now we're going to go over games."

"Great. Where are we throwing this shindig?" She took a seat beside Gabby and gave her a quick hug.

"Alicia's house," Gabby answered.

"Great." Elle pulled her pad out of her bag. "Since we figured out food last time, I went ahead and asked Miss Fern to make the cake."

"Perfect." Fawn smiled.

"I made a list of games I remember playing when we were in the hu...." Lily shook her head. "I mean, when we left here."

"You can say human." Gabby shrugged. "There is a huge difference. Even I see it. Plus, I'm a human. Besides, I only get a little shifter in me when Kru is randy."

Fawn groaned. "Such a bad pun."

Elle laughed. "Don't let him hear you call him

little."

Her cheeks turned pink. "Well, I do enjoy when he *proves* himself."

Lily sat back and watched her sisters interact. Tears blurred her eyes. What she wouldn't give to have her mom here to experience this all with them. Even for one day.

"Hey." Fawn touched her arm. "What's wrong?"

She shook her head and wiped her eyes. "Nothing. It's stupid." She cleared her throat. "Okay, so, moving on."

"What were the games?" Elle glanced up at Lily, pen poised to make notes.

"Guess what's in the diaper. Then slam a bottle of juice. There is also a blindfolded taste test. Guess the size of the baby bump. You have to use toilet paper and see how many squares it'll take to wrap around their belly. Pin the pacifier on the baby. Baby shower bingo."

Fawn's brows furrowed. "How many should we choose?"

"I think each one I went to had about four games then present opening and cake."

"Four games it is." Gabby smacked her knee. "You'd think I would have participated in these things, but old ladies don't invite sweet butts or the president's little sister to their little soirees."

"What's a sweet butt?" They'd never asked Gabby about her life before she came to them, especially after everything happened, but she was curious.

"Well, let's just say, they're only at the club for the perks, not for the long haul." She cleared her throat. "Sex. All the time. With multiple people. Whenever the guys want it. It's worse at parties."

Lily frowned. The more Gabby opened up to them about her past, the more she disliked the people who were supposed to be her family. "This is your day. So, you've got nothing to worry about anymore."

"I'm also making the invitations tonight," Elle stated. "Is there anyone else you'd like to add?"

Fawn and Gabby shook their heads. If some of the females of the pack weren't sure about going, they'd bring treats back for everyone, anyway. "Great. Then I think we've finally got everything organized." She let out a satisfied sigh. "Last thing to do is get both of you to Rapid City."

"Why?"

"To register for baby gifts. It's a human tradition. It gives people an idea of what you want and in what colors. It's supposed to be fun. Either the women go with their husbands or their friends."

Fawn gave her a curious glance. "When do you want to go?"

Lily snorted. "Whenever your mates will allow you out of their grasps, and preferably when they're busy and don't know what we're doing."

Gabby chuckled. "Good luck. Kru still won't allow me out of his sight for more than ten minutes."

"Don't worry, I've got a plan."

# Chapter Three

A week had gone by since his incident with Lily. He hadn't had time to think about a plan, let alone implement it.

As Chris drove down the state route back to Los Lobos, he knew his time was running short. *A mate is a mate, is a mate.* Though he repeated the mantra, he couldn't help but worry. Did he have it wrong? Could the kiss they shared be just a kiss?

His wolf growled, the hackles on the back of his neck rising. The wild part of him didn't agree with his assessment. Yet, the human side demanded he continue to take his time. He'd never force someone, let alone Lily, to do anything they didn't want. Mating was a life commitment. An unbreakable bond. He'd seen it day after day with his parents.

When Henry twirled his mom around in a circle after dinner the night before, he'd sworn thirty years disappeared right before his eyes. Shortly thereafter, he left, giving the mated pair the time they needed on their own. Chris wanted the same. Desperately.

Didn't Lily see the same with her brothers?

Fawn's mated sister? Didn't she see the love in their eyes when they gazed at their mates? He did.

He yearned for the same. Could taste it. In those moments, he wanted to gather Lily in his arms and prove to her how good it could be.

In the distance, town came into focus. Life carried on down there. Reborn in love, not hate. He had to convince his potential mate to give him a shot. Yet, no matter how many times his thoughts circled, he was no closer to an answer. Then a devious idea took root, and anticipation filled him. Sometimes, the best way to catch prey was to lay a trap. Oh yeah, there was no way in hell she'd ever be able to say no or ignore them being mates.

Instead of going home, he turned off onto the main road into town. He didn't think Lily, for all her sass and bluster, could be a full-time submissive. And, for all his Dominant tendencies, he didn't think he could handle someone being dependent on him twenty-four hours a day.

On the other hand, playing, making it fun, pushing boundaries; he was all for it. He'd make his saucy little she-wolf crave his touch. His adrenaline spiked and excitement raced through his body. Chris parked out front of the convenient store then got out of his truck.

For his encounter with Lily, he wanted everything to be brand new. Fresh rope, a bandanna. Spring clamps. Sure, all of his purchases were a little modified, and, yes, he had everything he needed in his kit, but the life he had in Wyoming and the one he had here were two different things.

Even though he interacted with the human world on a daily basis, it wasn't where he belonged, so he'd shucked those things he'd procured there, and went with a simple pack life in Los Lobos. Here, he wasn't Chris the Dom and veterinarian. He was Chris, son to Henry and Fern, and a vet.

He waved to the clerk then made his way back to the hardware section in the store. He needed at least two twelve-foot bundles of rope, eight inches of beaded chain, and the clamps. On the way to the counter, he grabbed a light-blue calico-print bandanna. It matched Lily's country charm. He placed his items next to the register and waited as the clerk rang it up.

"Trying something new?"

Chris quirked a brow. "I'm sorry?"

"With Kalum's cattle. I heard he had some wayward calves up there the other day." The man continued to write down the prices of his purchases.

"Oh." He laughed. "Yeah, something like that."

"It'll be seventeen dollars and forty-five cents."

Chris pulled a twenty out of his wallet. "Keep the change." He grabbed the bag on the counter.

"Good luck."

"Thanks." He'd need it.

He placed the bag into the utility box attached to the bed of his pickup then climbed into the driver's seat.

Before heading home, he thought he'd make a quick stop. He'd found out from Elle a few days ago Lily had started taking Jordan to the park in the afternoons.

Jordan's newest friend happened to be a precocious and cute-as-a-button six-year-old. Jessie hadn't been a part of the pack for very long, but she sure had caught the attention of the other members and had Caleb Burrows, Hannah's mate, wrapped securely around her little finger. Now it seemed, Jordan had been wrapped around the other.

Caleb had even petitioned Drew for permission to build a small agility course for the kids—all Jessie's idea. Within weeks a crew had cleared five hundred square feet near the center of town and installed balance beams, monkey bars, and rope ladders. Soon they would add pegged walls for climbing and over/under obstacles, perfect to help the kids learn how limber their little bodies were.

He slowed as he came around the curve. Lily sat on the bench handcrafted by Brick Northridge, the pack's resident carver and furniture maker. Hannah Burrows, one of the newer human packmates sat next to her. Some kids were climbing across the monkey bars while others played on the balance beam.

Parked, he climbed out and strolled toward the playground, watching the kids as he went.

"Come on, Jordan, keep up." Jessie nimbly worked her way across the equipment.

"I'm right behind you," he growled, tapping her swinging foot with his own.

The girl giggled as she quickened her pace. "Last one across is a rotten egg."

"Then you're going to be stinky," Jordan challenged.

They jumped down and ran to the rope ladders. The way the girl kept glancing back at the boy with such adoration, as though he could do no wrong in her book, and vice versa, had him a bit curious. Mates knew mates. *Nah.* He brushed off the idea and strolled over to where Hannah and Lily sat.

"I swear she's going to rule the roost one day."

Hannah laughed as she glanced down at a sleeping Micha in her arms.

"I believe Jordan is more than happy to help her out." Lily shook her head. "I've witnessed a lot of things in my life, but these two are joined at the hip."

Both kids turned and waved at them, their cheeks pink from playing, their brows wet with sweat. Both appeared to be enjoying themselves immensely.

"They're happy. Hannah, Lily." Chris tipped his hat at them. "May I join you?"

The women exchanged looks then Hannah smiled. "You know, I just remembered Birdie needed my and Jessie's help this afternoon. How about I take Jordan with me, and I'll let Tinks know to pick him up in a couple of hours at the diner?"

Since Will and Birdie had arrived in town with Hannah and Jessie, they'd rebuilt the old diner, which had been renamed Dottie's, and had a small but steady clientele. The place looked nothing like it had, and it was okay by him. Plus, he liked the old couple. They were pretty level-headed about the whole shifting idea—which surprised him, but shouldn't have. His mom read books written by a human who made his heroes wolves.

"Sounds great. We won't be long." Chris grinned.

Lily crossed her arms, pushing her perky breasts up. A hint of her freckled flesh peeked out for his perusal. "She asked me, Chris. I am capable of answering questions."

Hannah smothered a laugh. "I'll see you soon. Tell Fawn I'd be honored to join you for the baby shower." The woman stood then called out to the kids. "We're leaving. Last one to the diner doesn't get a hot apple cider."

Jessie hollered and began to run, Jordan hot on her heels. "I'm going to win," she cried out.

Amused by the display, he sat beside Lily and laid his hand on her knee. The kids were so open. Free. Able to show themselves without fear. Drew brought back security and happiness to the pack. It was part of their healing.

"Those two are going to keep us on our toes," he whispered, as Hannah draped her arm over Jessie's shoulder, while the little girl held onto Jordan's hand as though it were a lifeline.

"Tell me about it. They've been this way since they met at school."

"And here I thought he didn't have many friends."

Lily laughed. "He has quite a few, according to Tinks."

He motioned toward the kids. "Do you think?"

"They're mates?" Lily shrugged. "I don't know. It could be the novelty of being here. Or puppy love."

"Yeah, I thought the same, however...."

Lily glanced up at him. "Say no more."

"Mum's the word." He mimed zipping his lips.

She scrunched up her nose, crinkling the freckles on the bridge. "Anyway, what did you need to talk to me about?"

"I want one night with you."

"Excuse me?" Incredulousness filled her tone.

"There you go again, jumping to conclusions."

"I think spending one night with you is pretty self-explanatory." She frowned. The scent of anger and disbelief tinged the scent of intrigue. He'd have missed it if he hadn't been paying attention.

"It's not what you think, Lily." Well, it kind of

was, but not in the same context as it sounded. "You and I both know we're mates and we're fighting a losing battle."

"Says who?" For all her bluster, the sweet, timid scent of her arousal swirled around him.

"Do you really want to go there?"

"Fine. So we're mates. Doesn't mean I want to consummate it. For all you know, I have other suitors vying for my hand."

Chris growled and lunged toward her, stopping mere inches from her face. Lily's breath hitched, and the pulse at her neck twitched. "Don't push me. I'm hanging on by a thread as it is. I've been good about this. Giving you the time you needed because I won't force you. However, saying stupid shit, will get you turned over my knee and your ass spanked."

"Asshole!" Lily balled up her fists and punched at his chest. "Brute! How dare you talk to me like I'm some object you can tell what to do."

*Fuck.*

Anger surged through her, darkening the taste of her desire clinging to the air around them. His dick throbbed. His wolf tensed, waiting for her next move—daring her to run, so he could give chase.

Chris grabbed her wrists and lowered them until they were secured behind her back. Her breathing became rapid. Oh yeah, she got off on this. He smirked. "Admit it, Lily, you like this."

"I'll admit to nothing."

If he allowed it, she'd go down fighting him tooth and nail. Chris bent to nuzzle her neck. "This battle will only make the need burn brighter. Haven't you wondered what it will feel like when I mark you?" He nipped the juncture of her shoulder and throat.

"Chris." She let out a shuddered exhale.

"Shh," he whispered. "I've got you."

"I don't think—"

"Then don't think," he coaxed. "Isn't it time to start *your* life with *your* mate?"

She withdrew from his embrace, and he let go of her hands. "I'm afraid."

Chris tucked a finger beneath her chin and tipped her face up. "Of what, she-wolf?"

"Failing."

He snorted. "There's no way in hell you'll ever disappoint me." For all her bristling, she still reminded him of a timid wolf, needing a little more praise to bring her out of her shell.

"When?"

"When what?"

"When do you want me to spend one night with you?"

"When you're ready. You can tell me." Giving her the power to come to him might be like shooting himself in the foot. Yet, for as much as he wanted her with him, he'd still give her the ability to make her own decisions on her timeframe. He only hoped it wouldn't blow up in his face.

"Okay."

Chris gathered her in his arms and hugged her tight. "You won't regret this."

# Chapter Four

Lily couldn't get the predatory look in Chris's eyes out of her mind as she sat on her favorite bench in the agility area for the kids. For two days, she'd thought about what he said and how she'd felt the minute he trapped her against the bench. An excited thrill had raced down her spine, and her hussy-of-a-wolf perked up.

Though her body responded to his heady scent— a mixture of leather and wilderness—his words penetrated her soul. Maybe she had hidden within her familial ranks, taking care of everyone so she didn't have to venture out on her own. She'd been telling him the truth when she'd admitted she was scared.

A gust of cool fall air blew through the hills, causing the trees to sing their sad song of bramble branches knocking together. The scent of snow clung to the air as she pulled her favorite shawl, one her mother made when Lily was little, tighter around her shoulders. Almost a year ago, she'd kissed Chris under the mistletoe. Her body warmed at the memory and pushed back the chill.

The sensation of the ground dropping out from under her feet shot through her, leaving her lightheaded and giddy. A rush of adrenaline bubbled up, and she swore she could feel his lips on hers. The powerful connection between them had left her reeling. *Mate.*

Yeah, he was the one for her, but giving over to it was another story.

Another whip of cold wind pushed a lock of hair into her eye. She pushed it behind her ear and sighed. Chris was right. She deserved what her siblings had. Love. Happiness. A sense of purpose and belonging—besides taking care of her family. Still a niggle of self-doubt swamped her. Who'd be there to pick her up if she fell? At least when Kalum decided to pursue Fawn, she and Graham had been there every step of the way.

And, though their courtship had been a little...different, she and Kalum had helped Graham and Elle. They even helped Kru with Gabby. Who'd support her? Who did she turn to when she had questions or struggled with the decision in general?

In the last few months, she'd begun to wonder if maybe she'd end up alone. Everyone else had mated, so why did it matter if she floundered? She'd given plenty of pep talks, yet she had no one to return the favor.

While watching Jordan and Jessie play, she still didn't know what to do about Chris. In times like these, she'd tell Kalum to take the bull by the horns, or she'd tell Graham to shape up and settle down. What would they say to her? Did they even care what happened?

"Jordan, you're supposed to chase me," Jessie called out.

"Not if it means you might get hurt." He strode to where Jessie hung from the rope ladder. "My mom taught me to protect womenfolk. You're a woman, too, so I won't ever put you in danger."

Lily snickered a little. He had a fierce protective streak along with a natural ability with animals. "He's right, Jessie."

"Ah man," she whined, climbing down.

"I brought us a treat." Jordan distracted the downtrodden girl. "Momma made it." He pulled two pieces of dried meat out of his back pocket. "It's real deer. Douglas caught it out on the trail. You should have seen how big it was. My aunt Bobbi is making me a blanket from his hide."

"But it's been in your pocket." Jessie wrinkled her nose.

"Eat it," Jordan prodded. "It'll put fur on your chest."

"But, I don't want fur on my chest."

"You're a wolf, aren't you?" Jordan leaned in. "We all got fur on our chests. This will make it look cooler."

"I don't know." Jessie turned the jerky this way and the other. "Deer are friends of mine, and I don't think it's a good idea to—"

Jordan took a bite of his and grinned. "Best buck ever. Come on, Jessie, try it. If you take a bite, I'll do whatever you want for the rest of the afternoon."

"Really?" The little girl got a devious look in her eyes.

"Yep, wolf's honor."

"Okay." She took a bite out of the dried meat.

"Mmm, this is good."

"Told ya. My mom is the best."

"Lily?" Jessie called out. "Can we go get some of my dolls? I want to play dress up, since Jordan promised to do whatever I wanted if I ate the dried deer meat."

His mouth fell open, and his eyes grew wide. He began to sputter out an answer, but couldn't say anything.

Lily smothered her laugh, allowing him to squirm a little bit longer before helping him out. "How about later? It's almost time to meet your mom, anyway."

"You owe me, Jordan." Jessie took another bite of her treat. "Big time."

By the time she dropped Jessie and Jordan off, Lily had been nowhere near answering the questions swirling in her mind. As she stepped up onto the porch, laughter filtered outside.

She entered to find Fawn curled up in her favorite spot on the couch, Kalum lounging beside her. Graham and Elle sat on the love seat.

"Did you have fun?" Fawn rubbed her burgeoning belly.

A pulse of envy crept through her. "We did. I think Jordan's plan backfired on him, though."

"What did he do?" Graham gave her a curious look.

"He stopped Jessie from getting hurt."

"He did? What happened?" Elle's tone became serious.

"She decided to put herself in a precarious spot, and Jordan didn't like it. So, he helped her down and shared his jerky with her." She took the empty seat across from them. "But not before she balked at him and it."

Graham quirked his brow. "Why didn't she want to try it?"

"It's deer."

Kalum chuckled.

"So, he bargained with her. He said he'd do whatever she wanted if she tried the deer meat."

Fawn sat forward slightly. "What does he have to do?"

"Play dress up with her dolls."

Elle and Fawn laughed.

"I heard Chris came to see you," Fawn interjected. "What did he want?"

She glanced between her and her brothers. "How...how did you know?"

Graham laughed. "Your little scene with Chris in the play area is the talk of the town."

*Well, so much for easing into this conversation.* "He asked me out."

"Finally." Kalum hit his knee. "What did you say?"

She shrugged and looked away.

"Why don't we start with why you didn't you tell us?"

Lily nibbled on her thumb while staring out over the pastureland through the bay window. Cows mulled around chewing on cud or eating grass. "You've been busy."

"We're never too busy for you," Fawn whispered.

"How long, Lily?" Graham glanced up at her.

She shook her head. "Years, I guess. Since we were kids."

"Wait." Kal held up his hand. "He's a good twelve

years older than you."

"Yeah. Your point?"

"You were only fourteen when we left," Graham muttered.

"I'm confused." Elle frowned. "Are you saying she did something inappropriate at fourteen? Because if I remember correctly...."

"No," Graham added quickly. "I figured she'd be into boys, not...men."

Humiliation rolled through her. She'd seen Chris, laughed at one of his corny jokes while he worked on the farm with Kalum. On one particularly hot July afternoon, she'd retreated to the cool, dark shade of the hay barn out back. Up in the rafters, she'd made a place for herself where she'd bring her prized books to read. Her mom even put together a little basket of goodies. Dried meats, cheeses, and jams. She also had biscuits and sweet tea.

While nestled up there, she heard Kal and Chris come back from the field. Their dad had bailed the hay early in the morning, so they had to store it. Some they'd use for feed, the rest they'd sell or give to those who needed it most. As Chris stepped into the dimly lit space, he pulled his shirt off and threw it over the angled support post.

*"Damn, I didn't think it'd get so hot out there."* *He took a long pull from a jug of water. The muscles of his back rippled and flexed. His sweat-slick flesh glistened in the shafts of sunlight coming through the small port windows below her perch.*

*"We'll hit the waterhole later, maybe find a little fun." Her brother took the water from his friend.*

*"I wouldn't mind getting to know Stacy a little*

better." Chris turned to the side, and she got her first glimpse of his washboard abs.

Her mouth watered. She swore she had heart palpitations. And her wolf? The little horndog wanted to rub all over him. Mark him with her scent so he couldn't touch anyone else. The irrational thought surprised her. It also scared her. She didn't understand.

"I wonder if the Hawthorne girl will be there. I had Momma bring some food for her and her brother, but the kid refused then hurried Momma away from their front door."

"The boy is skinny as a rail." Chris grunted. "I thought Gill was supposed to be taking care of them."

"Lily Rose," her mom called out. "Darn girl."

She scrambled back away from the ledge and unfortunately kicked her pencil tin over, drawing her brother and Chris's attention. "Mrs. Truesdale. I believe I've found the little she-wolf."

Her mom's curvy form filled the barn. She placed her hands on her hips; the dishtowel she always seemed to carry with her flapped in the light breeze. Her long brown hair had been pulled back in the tight bun she wore whenever she cooked. "Did you lose track of time?"

Heat suffused her cheeks. "Sorry, Momma." She scrambled down the steps. With her hands full, the trip was precarious to say the least. As she positioned her foot on the fourth rung from the bottom, she slipped. The sensation of free-falling startled her, and she gasped.

"I got you." Chris's warm embrace wrapped around her as he set her down. "You all right?" His *brilliant smile momentarily left her awestruck.*

*"Y-yeah." Her words had been a little bit breathier than necessary. "Thanks."*

*"Not a problem."*

*"Girl, you are going to give me and your father a heart attack before we're old enough." Her mom wrapped her arm around Lily's shoulder. "Dinner will be ready in an hour, boys, Make sure you're both cleaned up and presentable."*

*A chorus of, "Yes, ma'am," filled the space.*

*When they were outside, Lily mumbled, "Sorry, Momma. I didn't realize I'd been outside for so long."*

*"A girl's place isn't spying in a barn and staring at men she shouldn't be looking at."*

*"Oh, but...I wasn't. They just showed up."*

*Her mom laughed. "You have a lot to learn, young lady. A lot to learn."*

"Wait, so you noticed him then?" The edge in Graham's voice surprised her.

"I guess so." She shrugged. "I never thought anything of it, and, soon after, we were gone. It's not like I totally understood it, nor had a chance to, either."

"You've been distant since we got back," Kal stated. "Why?"

"Females talk, dear brother. They're also not kind."

"Fuck." Graham snarled. "Which ones?"

"Does it matter?"

"I think what your brother is trying to say is, he's sorry you went through hell because of some petty women." Elle elbowed him.

"Wow, you learned Neanderthal quickly."

33

Her mated sister laughed. "Kind of have to since the Truesdale men seem to be fluent."

"Lily," Fawn started, "what can we do to help?"

"I don't think you can. I have to wrap my mind around his offer and give him an answer."

"Don't wait." Graham took Elle's hand in his. "Trust me. I spent too much time waiting to die, when I should have been preparing for my mate." The tragedy of it all was the fact everyone had assumed Elle had died the night Greer, one of Magnum's henchmen, murdered her parents and set her house on fire. But Ryker had arrived and killed Greer. Then, doing his best to carry out her parents' wishes to keep her safe, he'd made it look like she'd died, too, by throwing Greer's body in the fire. The minute she stepped into town and back into Lily's brother's life, a new light had filled him. The sour demeanor and distant behavior had disappeared, replaced with a zest for life.

Kal inclined his head. "Yep. Grab onto this with both hands, Lily. We'll be right here to catch you if you ever fall. I promise."

# Chapter Five

For a minute, Chris thought he'd gone insane. One day turned into three then a week. He began to lose hope. Maybe he'd gone about this all wrong. Perhaps even his wolf had it wrong.

Then, Lily found him at The Den, and said yes. She didn't stay to talk or grab a beer. She simply gave him her answer and walked back out the door. It happened so fast, he had to ask Paul if she'd really been there and if she'd really said yes to him.

The mute omega who worked at Gee's bar grinned then patted him on the shoulder before strolling off. Ever since he mated PG, the guy seemed to bloom right in front of the pack. Everyone had started learning sign language just so they could talk with a man who'd been silent for so long.

When Chris arrived at the Truesdale house, Kalum waited for him. If he meant to deter Chris, he wouldn't put up with it. Lily belonged with him. "Kalum."

"Chris." His friend flicked his gaze toward the pasture. "I suppose you're here because of Lily?"

"'Spose I am. I don't want a fight."

"Who says we will?" Kal pushed off his truck and sauntered over to him. "She's nervous. Graham and I have been wrapped up in our lives as of late and we haven't paid her any mind."

Like he hadn't noticed. "Understandable. You're both newly mated. You have a baby on the way, and Graham and Elle are reconnecting after all this time. Can't be easy."

"Yeah, well, I think Lily made it too easy on us. In fact, I know she did."

"It's her disposition. She's taken over for your mom."

Kal nodded. "I saw it, too, when we moved back and then when she helped me with Fawn. The girl is the spitting image of our mother, not only in looks but in her disposition. She needs to explore life."

"I mean to explore it with her. She's my mate." For some inexplicable reason, he had to reaffirm his position with Lily.

"How long have you known? No more bullshitting."

"I'd say the kiss under the mistletoe last year, but I have had a sneaky suspicion for a long-ass time." Since she'd gone from cute little Lily Rose Truesdale, to the pretty little teen, and now the woman who had the ability to steal his breath.

"Figured as much." Kal grunted. "She said since the day in the barn."

Chris's brows rose. Curiosity filled him. "Which day?"

Kal recounted the day Lily fell off the ladder rung. Along with their conversation and how damn hot it had been. *Shit. Way to screw with a guy's ability to think.*

"She said it started then, but she didn't understand and we left soon afterwards."

"I don't know what to say," Chris admitted.

"Didn't think you would. She left all of us speechless, too."

"She's afraid, isn't she?" he hedged.

"No doubt. She's doing something for herself for the first time. Everything has been done for us. I think she thought she'd be doing this on her own, too."

When Kal finally left, Chris contemplated calling this whole thing off. The pressure she'd put on herself along with his own worries made him second-guess himself. What if she didn't like his idea? Where did it leave them? Could he go back to a vanilla life without acknowledging his baser needs?

Even if he didn't think he could, he'd have to. *A mate is a mate.* He'd never give her up...even if she didn't like to be spanked or tied up.

# Chapter Six

"Are you sure you have everything you need?" his mother asked for the hundredth time since he'd stopped in for breakfast.

"Yes. Lily will be by the house tonight for dinner. I've got everything ready for her."

"Remember, slow and steady wins the race," his dad added. "When she's ready, Lily will let you know."

The one day he put himself on call for emergencies only, he made the mistake of coming home and finding his parents. "I know, Pops. My intentions are for her to see what our lives together could be like. Afterward, it's up to her to make the final decision."

"She'll come around." His mom patted his hand.

He was optimistic about it.

After he finished his breakfast, he decided to go for a run in the hopes the fresh air would do him some good. The woods behind his parents' place had been perfect for him to roam when he was old enough to shift and go it alone. Walking outside, he glanced out at the wide-open space and took a deep breath. Pine and wet earth greeted him. Once he disrobed, he allowed the shift to come over him.

When his feet touched the ground, he took off, galloping through the tall grass for the crop of trees directly in front of him. The smell of small game overrode the familial scent of his family's property.

He climbed deep into the Black Hills, seeking solitude for a few hours.

On his way home, he refined his plan. The quick, "Here is the plan, and this is what you'll wear for me. Now, change," wouldn't work for her. She'd throw everything back at him and laugh before walking out on him. He needed to be subtle. Ease her into the idea. Build trust between them.

In order for Lily to accept his home as hers, she would have to have her own space. She would have to know he wanted her. So, as he wound his way back down through the hills to his mother's house, he decided to spruce up his place a little, make her feel welcome. He stepped back up onto the porch, allowed the shift to come over him then glanced over his shoulder. His hackles bristled as though he were being watched. He waited a beat, uncaring of his nakedness.

Chris lifted his head and sniffed. The aroma of lilacs and wilderness greeted him. Then, through the line of trees, a small brindle-colored wolf appeared. Watched him. He made no move to cover up. *Lily.* He smirked as he placed his hands on his hips. The wolf blinked. Her ears twitched back and forth as though listening to everything around her.

"What are you doing?" he whispered.

The wolf's keen gaze locked with his. Then, in a blur of motion, she shifted and stood before him. Her long, curly brown hair hung loosely around her shoulders and brushed the tips of her rosy nipples. He salivated.

Her arms hung at her sides, exposing every inch of her slender form to his perusal. His groin tightened. Lily gave no indication of shyness. She also made no move to close the distance. She continued to stare at him. None of it made sense.

The seconds of their standoff ticked by. Her heated stare bored into him, twisting his guts. Their deadlock dragged on. Lily licked her lips, and a growl rumbled at the back of his throat. Did she even know she challenged him? Chris took a step forward. His body tensed with expectancy. If she ran, would he give chase? Should he?

Lily took a step backward. Her gaze darted from side to side—he assumed she was trying to figure the easiest way out of there. He'd always find her. She couldn't hide on his land.

He held himself, waiting for her next move. In a blur of light, she shifted then bolted for the thicket. His beast roared in outrage when he didn't move.

She needed time still. Needed to reconcile her newly forming life with him. Turning from the field, he reached for his clothes. As much as he'd love to give chase, he had stuff to do. Later, he'd ask her about this little show she put on for him. Later, he'd teach her what happened when she tempted the beast.

The day had been more productive than he'd Expected. After seeing Lily out behind the house, he went to Rapid City to grab a few things for his place.

The image of her poised there like some modern-day Lady Godiva made concentrating hard while he picked up what he needed. Questions swirled through his head. The biggest one, what had she been thinking?

When he returned to his house, he carried all of the bags into his room and placed them on his bed. He made room in his closet for her things then walked into his bathroom. He cleaned off a spot on the counter in the bathroom for her products, if she had any. She didn't seem like someone who'd have a shit ton of stuff; nevertheless, he'd give her the room she needed. In his bedroom sat a brand new walnut dresser he'd bought for her.

He'd also bought them a new bed along with new linens and comforters. He removed his name from the list of available Doms at the Dungeon, the small club nestled near the hills, as well. No point in poking his nose where it didn't belong...for now. When Lily felt ready, if ever, then he'd ease her into the lifestyle and the club. Until then, he didn't want the distraction of needy subs—there were more than a few. To put it nicely, they were the cheap whiskey and she was top shelf. Smooth as silk and went down easy.

In the living room, he built her a bookcase. She loved to read, even though she didn't tell anyone. With Kole Silver, the co-owner of Los Lobos Books and More's help, he filled some of the shelves with the genres she liked and set up an open tab at the bookstore in her name. The kitchen had all the latest and greatest cooking utensils for her since she loved to cook and bake.

With Fawn's help, after he spoke with Kal, he

digitized all of Lily's mom's recipes onto a tablet, and, thanks to Roland helping boost the pack's Internet and cell coverage, he also added a few new things she might want to try. In a few short days, his house went from being a bachelor pad to a mated home.

Once he'd finished putting everything away and had made sure the space looked presentable, he headed for the kitchen. The ingredients for their dinner waited on the counter. Chris washed his hands then set to work. Before long, the aroma of cooked deer sausage, peppers, and mushrooms permeated the air. Water boiled in the stockpot on the stove, and he added the uncooked pasta to it. Within a few minutes, he had everything put together and into the oven to finish cooking.

By the time he had taken a quick shower and changed, the timer went off.

He placed the glass casserole dish on a potholder then grabbed the salad Elle had made to save time and placed it next to the ziti. A quick glance at the clock let him know he had about fifteen minutes before she'd be there.

Nervous energy built inside him. He knew the plan by heart and understood, without a shadow of a doubt, none of it would scare her off. However, the niggle of what-if raised the fine hairs on the back of his neck. *What if this all blows up in my face?*

\*\*\*

"This is such a bad idea," Lily mumbled for no less than the third time while being primped and dressed for her "big date" with Chris.

Since she'd vomited up all of her secrets to her

family, they never left her alone. They took some of her chores away from her so she could prepare for her encounter—which led to her stupid stunt at Fern and Henry's place earlier that morning.

Coming out of the woods like she had and seeing a gloriously naked Chris—his flexed back exposing the taut muscles of his shoulders—her gaze lowered to his butt, and she'd near about swallowed her tongue. If she'd thought at her tender age of fourteen the man had been built, seeing him now...sheesh. She felt lightheaded—the sound of her heart pounded in her ears. A little...a lot overwhelmed. Then he'd turned to face her. His legs were spread shoulder width apart, his shaft engorged. Dear Lord, the man was hung. Thick and long. A twinge of worry had filled the pit of her stomach.

He'd devastated her willpower with his smirk, but the intensity in his gaze held her stock still. Then he'd taken a step toward her. Her heart pounded. Her hands grew slick with sweat. She didn't know what to do. So, like any other brave female ensnared by her potential mate, she ran. Hard and fast for home.

"No, it's not a bad idea." Fawn interrupted her thoughts. "You're nervous. You have every right to be. I can't tell you how anxious I was right before the Winter Solstice celebration. I thought my stomach would come tumbling out of my mouth before Kalum showed up."

"I thought Kru might kill me the minute he showed up at the hotel," Gabby added from where she sat on Lily's bed.

"If you've forgotten, I returned from the dead," Elle stated. "We've all been there, and so have countless others in the pack who've been in your shoes."

Lily frowned. "What if I'm making this out to be more than it is?"

"More than it is?" Fawn laughed. "It doesn't get much bigger than finding your mate, sweetheart."

She had a point. "I have the potential to make a fool out of myself."

"We all did." Elle came up behind her and laid her hand on Lily's shoulder. "I came home certain I had it all figured out. Graham picking me up shot the idea to shit. It all comes down to two things. Whether you're a fool because you're being mean and don't want to be there, or you're doing it because you're so nervous and it happens."

Fawn turned the chair back toward the mirror. "What do you think?"

Her curly hair had been pulled back into a half-updo. Her makeup enhanced her features. Her slate-colored eyes glowed with anticipation. What did she think? "Wow. I really wish my mom was here to witness this."

Her heart squeezed.

"She is." Gabby squeezed her shoulder. "I believe all our parents are."

Like her, Gabby had lost both of her parents at a young age. Tears welled up in her eyes. "Oh no! If I cry, I'll make a mess of everything." Lily gave a watery laugh as she grabbed a tissue. "I can't say thank you enough for everything all of you have done."

"You don't have to thank us." Fawn smiled. "We're family. We're supposed to take care of each other."

"I think we should wrap this up. The guys are

waiting downstairs. Up with you now." Gabby motioned for Lily to stand. "We need to see the whole ensemble."

She stood then stepped away from the mirror. "What do you think?"

Elle, with Kizzy in tow, and she had gone to Rapid City the day before and bought her a pretty little summer dress. The scoop-neck bodice complemented the knee-length skirt and had been done in a pretty floral print.

"Stunning." Fawn sighed wistfully. "You're going to knock his socks off."

Lily studied her reflection in the mirror. She didn't look like herself. Older, a bit wiser, perhaps. Sometimes, she felt as though everyone saw her as a kid still, not a grown woman, and maybe she saw herself the same way.

Until today.

"He's going to be tripping over himself tonight," Elle added.

"And if he doesn't," Gabby interjected, "I'll get Hombre and Blackjack after him."

She laughed. "I'll remember that, just in case."

She hugged each of her mated sisters then took a

deep breath. "It's now or never."

# Chapter Seven

Lily stepped up to Chris's door and knocked. His lands were open with tons of room to run if he wanted. The house, though small, was new. She wondered if perhaps Ross built the place for Chris after he came home.

Not fancy by any means, it did give off a homey vibe. Welcoming in the masculine touches. Above the door hung a right-side-up horseshoe, ensuring prosperity and luck for those who entered the home. Across from her, a porch swing swung in the gentle breeze. Would they sit there in the future, watching their children then grandchildren play?

The thought, though odd, felt right. Like she stood where she was supposed to be. All the questions and doubts swirling in her mind for the last few weeks disappeared. She raised her hand to knock on the door at the same moment it opened, and there stood Chris.

Her breath left her in a rush. Dressed in dark denim jeans, a long-sleeve shirt, and a pair of brand new boots, his easy smile melted her heart. A glimmer of heat filled his whiskey-hued eyes, and her heart went on a wild gallop. "Hi," she murmured.

"Hi." His gaze touched every inch of her body. He waited a beat, ramping up the adrenaline already banging around inside her before stepping aside. "Want to come in?"

"Sure." She took a deep breath. This was it.

Lily stepped over the threshold, and her mouth watered. The sweet, spicy scents of Italian food mingled with garlic bread. Her stomach growled with appreciation. "I'm going to pretend you didn't hear that."

Chris laughed as he placed his hand on the small of her back and directed her toward the small dining area off the living room. Everything inside his house had a masculine quality to it. A leather couch sat in front of a handcrafted coffee table. A cowhide throw lay on the floor in front of the river-rock fireplace.

In the dining room, a small round dinner table had two places already set. All of the walls were painted a neutral color, a mix of sand and taupe. She figured he'd have painted them in dark greens or black-ish. Several of Tinks' paintings hung there as well.

"I like what you've done with the place." Nervous energy crept through her.

"Thanks. Ross is the man. I told him what I wanted and boom"—he motioned to the house—"he delivered. I have three bedrooms, two bathrooms. I have a special tech room in case an injured pet shows up, and something extra."

"I'd love to see the rest of your home."

He winked. "I'll give you the grand tour of the place when we're finished with dinner."

She sat in the chair he pulled out for her. "Thank you."

"Welcome, and it's our house, Lily." He returned to the kitchen and reappeared a moment later with a casserole dish. "I built this when I knew what I wanted."

His meaning hadn't been lost on her. "Oh," she mumbled. "Kind of putting the cart before the horse here, aren't you?"

Chris grinned, the fine age lines crinkling at the corners of his eyes, giving him a more rugged appearance. *Be still my beating heart.*

"Nope. I have a good feeling about this." He made one more trip to the kitchen then grabbed the bottle of wine sitting on the table. "I thought we could...celebrate a little."

"This is all too much, Chris. I'm a simple girl. You're treating this as though we're millionaires."

"Not quite millionaires. But I have been working a long time and saving the majority of the money I made. I don't charge the pack large sums of money, but the ranches and patrons surrounding us make up for what I do here." He plated up some of the salad. "Besides, spoiling you will be my pleasure."

"I don't want to be spoiled."

"Not even a little?" He added some of the pasta he'd made for them onto her plate.

She shook her head. "Momma always told me a woman's job is to take care of her mate. It's our duty to be there for you. It's an important part of the pack dynamic. In return, our mate is supposed to be loyal and loving."

"Spoiling and being loyal aren't two mutually exclusive terms. There are several different meanings, in fact. Plus, every mating is different. Just depends on the couple."

Lily tilted her head to the side in contemplation. He had a point. She'd seen the differences in her family's matings. "Do you honestly want to spoil me?"

"Sometimes, like now."

She took a sip of the wine. The sweet tartness of the berries had a bit of a dryness in the aftertaste. She took another sip. "Okay." She placed the glass back on the table. "Will I get to do the same for you?"

"Spoil me?"

She nodded.

"Of course. I'd never turn you down."

"Can I be honest with you?" Lily stabbed a few noodles with her fork.

"I'd expect no less."

"Why do I feel like the other shoe is about to drop?"

He laughed. "Eat. You're going to need your strength tonight."

"You didn't answer my question." She took a bite of the food he'd prepared and moaned. "My compliments to the chef."

He raised his glass. "As to your question, relax. There are no other shoes tonight, it's just us."

She cut her gaze to him but did as he requested. "What did you want to talk about?"

"I think it's self-explanatory, isn't it?"

"You tell me." The cat-and-mouse game they played only served to make her more nervous about their encounter.

"We're mates. We're destined by fate to live a long, loving life together."

"Potential mates," she corrected. "You've not

made it clear about our situation. To tell the truth, we've kissed a total of one time. After which, you never pursued anything else."

"Because you've been too stubborn. I've put myself in your way since last Christmas, and you've rebuked me every chance you got."

Neither completely true, nor a lie. She took another bite of her dinner, giving her time to formulate her answer. "You have other women. I've heard the females talk."

"Women will always talk. They get jealous. As a matter of fact, I haven't had anyone in my bed since I returned home."

"No, you take them to someplace called the Dungeon."

Chris placed his fork on the edge of his plate and sat back. "What do you know of the Dungeon?"

She shrugged. "Not much. I know you go there a lot. According to some of the women."

"Are you jealous?"

She snorted then laughed. "No. What do I have to be jealous of?"

He grunted. "Your potential mate screwing around on you, for starters."

"I already told you. Nothing is set in stone yet. If you'd rather seek the comfort of some hussy's open arms, go for it. More power to you."

Chris couldn't believe what he heard. Though the words came out of her mouth, it was as if someone else were saying them. Her slate-blue eyes cooled, as had her temperament.

He held her chilly stare. "I've never sought comfort from any hussy."

"And I'm a virginal, mystical wolf." Sarcasm dripped from her words.

"I'll bet you are. Tell me, Lily, what has your pretty panties in such a twist? Why are you trying to destroy this evening?"

"I'm not." She huffed. "I think we both deserve to have all our cards on the table before we take this to another level."

"Okay. So why are you throwing all my supposed indiscretions on the table as ammunition against me, when I've not done the same to you?"

She sniffed then turned her face away from his and looked out the dining room window. "Did Stacy show you a good time?"

He could lie and say yes, however, it would only add fuel to her fire. "What do you want me to say?"

"Why don't you start with the truth?"

"Which truth? Yours or mine?"

Lily crossed her arms and glared at him. Anger radiated off her in suffocating waves along with jealousy and a hint of curiosity. "There is only *the* truth."

Chris's hand curled into fists as he fought to control his temper. The stubborn set of her jaw coupled with the way she lifted her chin just so had his palms itching to spank the bullishness out of her.

She flipped his switch. The Dominant wolf inside him bristled at her tone and demanded he take her to task. Make her submit to her mate. "Stacy and I had fun."

"So you fucked her."

He made a noncommittal noise while lifting his shoulder. "Doesn't matter anymore."

"You did."

"You're jealous, she-wolf."

"No, I'm not."

Chris cocked a brow. "This time, when you say it, don't lie."

Lily pursed her lips and placed her napkin on the table. "I don't have patience for this nonsense. I believe it's time I leave."

He didn't move. For all her posturing, he'd hit the nail on the head. She'd known who he was meant to become at a young age and insomuch couldn't reconcile, even today, why they were in the position they were in.

"No, you aren't."

She snorted as she hurried out of the dining room. "Watch me, wolf. I don't need this, and I certainly don't need you."

"Careful, she-wolf." He growled, coming up behind her. "If you run out the door, I won't be responsible for what happens next."

Arousal tinged with a shred of fear wafted from her. His dick thickened behind the fly of his jeans as anticipation coursed through him.

*Run.*

He wanted her to. He craved chasing her through the hills before catching her and mounting her. The hedonistic, predatory thought did nothing to cool his already amped-up condition. In fact, it turned him on even more.

Lily hesitated. Her hand hovered inches over the doorknob.

His wolf pushed to the surface. His teeth elongated. His fur brushed at the back of his neck. "Run," he growled, his voice more of a wolf than of a man.

The erratic beat of her heart called to him as she licked her lips and glanced between him and the door. *Do it.* He willed her. The run would do both of them good. The other stuff could wait. Right now, his wolf needed her wolf's submission, and the only way to get it would be to give chase and give over to their basic needs.

Lily swung the door open, gave him one more curious look then took off, shifting mid-stride, and headed straight for the hills.

His wolf howled in triumph.

Chris gave chase, shifting as his foot hit the top step of his front porch. When he caught his little hellion, he'd show her what challenging the beast got her—*mated and fucked properly.*

# Chapter Eight

The soft plods of paws hitting packed dirt led Chris in the direction of his mate. Her subtle wild scent spurred him on. When he caught up to her, the things he'd do to her....

*Keep it cool. No need to freak her out.* Too late. She'd messed with the bull, and the time had come to show her the horns. Anticipation raced through him. In the last several weeks, the weather had turned decidedly colder. The below-freezing temperatures at night had left the ground hard and unyielding. Soon, snow would cover their trails, leaving them in a winter wonderland. Crazy how two years could change a person's perspective. Having Drew as their alpha had brought a lightness to their pack, something he never thought he'd get a chance to experience when he left all those years ago.

As he darted in and out of the brush, the aroma of her arousal grew thicker. He could taste it. *Fuck.* Lust pounded through his veins.

Chris kicked it up another notch and pushed through the thicket. There Lily stood, on a small ridge, her brindle-colored muzzle lifted toward the sky, steam rising off her back.

His breath caught.

Red with patches of black and light-tan fur sparkled in the moonlight. Her light-blue eyes glowed when a cloud covered the moon momentarily. Lily yipped then ambled down the rocky ledge. Her tail swished back and forth, teasing him as she went.

He snarled, crouching low. Whatever she'd planned for him, he'd be ready. He inched forward, sniffing the air as he went. When he got to the ledge, he followed the small path down to a clearing then waited.

It didn't take long for him to find Lily's scent, and he went for her. Bounding through the shrubbery while dodging trees and stumps, he searched for her. A few feet ahead of him, he caught a glimpse. She trotted down another path, almost as if she didn't have a care in the world. *Crazy she-wolf.*

Chris eased closer, watching where he put his feet so as not to make a sound. He came up behind her and growled before taking her to the ground. They tussled, fighting for dominance. Her little mouth grabbed at his front legs while she scratched at his belly.

Strong, for her size, she packed a punch. They rolled again, and his mouth wrapped around her throat. He added pressure. Little by little she relented until she stilled. Her soft whimper of acquiescence had him pulling back. Forcing her shift, he followed suit. Naked, he braced himself with his hands on either side of her arms.

Fire burned bright in her eyes. Her pulse hammered at her throat. "I've caught you."

"I let you," she replied.

"Sure, she-wolf."

She made a move to sit up, and he bared his teeth at her. "Let me go, Chris."

Watching her for a second, he grinned. "As you wish. Run, she-wolf."

She took off like a flash, back toward the house. He gave her a five second head start then hurried after her. She shuffled down the trail back to the house, her tail wagging back and forth as she balanced on the narrow path. Once she hit the even ground of the trail, she kicked it into high gear, putting distance between them.

She cut a swath through the woods and came out at the clearing near the back of his house then nimbly climbed the stairs. Chris made a running leap for the porch and shifted. Lily followed suit, and he caged her to the door. The need to claim her, to mark her so there'd be no doubt who she belonged to, filled him.

He leaned into her. "I'm trying to get some control here." Rubbing his cheek across hers, Chris sighed. He pressed a kiss to her forehead. "Do you know what you do to me? How much I crave you?"

"No, I don't."

He took her hand in his and lowered it to his straining erection. She wrapped her palm around his cock and gave a squeeze.

"Fuck." He grunted. His hips shifted, pushing into her grip. "This is what you do to me. You make me wild. You make me crave your touch in a way that scares me."

"Then maybe we shouldn't." She stroked him from tip to base.

His head fell back on his shoulders. "Oh I think

we should, she-wolf. You're really good at teasing me." Pushing open the back door, he shuffled them farther into the warm space. "Don't stop touching me." Her hand returned to his length, stroking him as he ran his hands over her flesh. "You're a treasure."

Her lips parted. A pink flush covered her chest, drawing his attention to her hard, strawberry-colored nipples. Small, and delicate, they called to him, tempting him to take a taste. A light dusting of freckles covered her flesh. He took in every curve and dip of her toned body, as he picked her up and carried her to the couch. Sitting down, he nipped her chin while breathing her in.

When he raised his gaze to hers, his nostrils flared. Desire curled in those beautiful blue orbs. It mingled with a timidness he coveted. "Am I your first?" he hedged while she continued to explore his length.

Crimson filled her cheeks, and she looked away. "No." She shook her head. "Not really."

This shy, demure Lily intrigued him. "Not really?" He skimmed his fingers down between her breasts and watched goose bumps form in his wake.

"Well, I've fooled around," she answered, squirming under his touch. "Why are you doing this to me?"

"Doing what?" he murmured, tracing the curve of her hip. She shuddered under his touch, her eyes dilated with arousal.

"Stop doing that."

"What?"

"Making my wolf feel like a bitch in heat," she grumbled. "It's disconcerting to say the least."

"She-wolf, we are in heat. Mating heat." Trailing

his finger over the juncture of her neck and shoulder, he stilled her hand. "I'll mark you here. Everyone will see it. They'll know my wolf is yours and yours is mine. "Then"—he touched her inner thigh—"I'll mark you here because I'm a possessive son of a bitch, and if anyone ever thinks of coming near your pussy, they'll know I claimed it and they're shit out of luck."

Lily's heart lodged in her throat. How had she gotten into this mess? "Chris I...." She swallowed whatever she'd been about to say when his hand cupped her sex. His deep, throaty groan did things to her. Naughty, delicious things. Things she didn't have a name for.

"You're wet," he crooned. Sitting forward slightly, his breath caressed her sensitive flesh, before his tongue swiped at her nipple.

Sparks ricocheted through her body, setting off mini orgasms. Her hips lifted of their own volition, desperate for his touch. His dark, rumbling chuckle startled her in the most sinful of ways.

*What the hell is wrong with me?*

"Please," she murmured.

No, wait. She hadn't meant to say please, had she? Didn't she mean stop? Let's talk more? Her breath hitched as he speared her with one of his broad fingers.

Chris cursed. The muscle in his jaw twitched. "Shit, you're tight." In a slow, methodical rhythm, he fingered her, opening her. "I'm never going to get enough of you, she-wolf."

She cried out and began pumping the hard flesh in her hand. His dick jumped. Lily ran her thumb over his slickened tip. She used the wetness to rub his glans and was rewarded with more of the sticky substance.

"Answer my question, Lily. Tell me the truth before I do something we'll both regret."

Regret? Right about now she'd ride him until the cows came home for all she cared. "Once. A long time ago before we came home. A-a boy from school." It had been more groping and fondling than the actual act of sex. Once he'd gotten inside of her and the initial pain disappeared, he'd only lasted long enough to gain his release. "It happened after Momma and Dad—"

"Shh. We'll take this slow and easy." He helped her straddle him. "You're going to sit on my lap."

She arched a brow. "Excuse me?"

Lifting her with ease, he placed her exactly where he wanted. The head of his erection slid through her folds and tapped her clit. "Like this." He groaned and palmed her ass, pulling her snug against him. "Then, I'm going to do this...."

He rolled her hips, before moving her up and down his cock. Pleasure fluttered low in her belly. Her eyes shut as she placed her hands on his shoulders. "Oh," she cried. Everything inside her tensed expectantly. "Feels good."

"It'll feel better when I'm in you."

"Do it," she whimpered.

"Not yet. I'm a big wolf, and I won't hurt you."

Up and down she went while he controlled the tempo. The maddening pace threatened to destroy her. How the hell did he expect her to keep going this way? Lily gasped and shivered in his arms. "Please."

"Almost." His breath brushed her sensitive

nipples before he drew the stiff peak into his mouth and sucked.

"Chris!" she sobbed. Her hips bucked against his as everything inside her detonated, shattering her.

"Now." He lifted her a bit then brought her back down on him. Her eyes went wide as he filled her.

Chris stretched her to capacity. With each thrust, he impaled himself more. Pleasure and pain mixed together in a heady cocktail. For long moments, she didn't know which way was up or her name. The intense feeling of coupling with her mate overwhelmed her.

When their thighs touched, he stilled. Every inch of her had been possessed by this man. Her gaze locked with his. It steadied her. The same violent emotions waging war inside her, reflected back at her. "I didn't know...." The husky quality of her voice surprised her.

"Neither did I," he murmured before kissing her. His tongue pushed into her mouth at the same second he began to rock her.

She moaned.

Tangling her tongue with his, she deepened the kiss, clinging to him as she swiveled her hips. The depth of her passion grew with each shift of their bodies. One of Chris's broad hands pressed to the middle of her back, holding her in place.

The wild animalistic sounds they made added to the heady atmosphere surrounding them. *This is mating. This is our souls combining.* Instinct told her, after today, things would change. Instead of being afraid, she wanted it.

Their cadence became erratic, his thrusts uneven. Bliss twined with lust and rushed through her system. The knot of pleasure in her lower belly grew, intensified, until she could only hold on for the ride and hope she'd garner some kind of relief.

"You're squeezing the fuck out of me, she-wolf." He groaned.

"It's too much," she sobbed, burying her face in his neck. The rapid beat of his heart called to her. Lily ran her tongue along the thin skin, and the desire to mark him only made the sensations crashing through her more severe.

Chris fit his hand between them and pushed her back slightly. His clever fingers found her clit, and she whined. So good—like a sundae covered in warm fudge and cherries. The change in angles also had the head of his cock rubbing a sensitive patch of nerves behind her clit.

Her eyes went wide.

"Do it. Let go. Give it to me, Lily. Your orgasms are mine."

His mouth latched onto her neck at the same moment his thumb pressed down on her clit. Her whole body went supernova. Searing pleasure shot through her. She heard someone screaming then quickly realized it was her as Chris growled and snarled, thrusting into her until his mouth covered her neck then bit down.

Another bliss-filled wave rolled through her when his teeth penetrated her flesh. She gave a weak moan as she rode out her climax and felt the wet heat of his release filling her. *Wow.* While in his arms, the world around them disappeared. With him, no one else mattered.

Limp and sated, he held her close. "You are fucking amazing, she-wolf." His arms tightened around her. "I'm never letting you go."

Good, because she'd never let him leave either. "Lucky for you, I feel the same way."

# Chapter Nine

Shafts of sunlight drifted through the curtains of his window and created a halo around his mate. *My mate....*

The golden light caught the hints of natural red-and-bronze highlights in her hair while darkening the sprinkle of freckles on her skin.

Content to stare at Lily, he watched her sleep, completely relaxed, trusting no one would do her any harm. Her features were soft. Her lips were still a bit swollen from their mating, and the mark at her neck glowed an angry shade of purple.

Chris had been a little rougher than he'd intended, but Lily took it. She surprised him with her appetite and aggressiveness. When she marked him, she struck fast. The mark on his pectoral muscle would show her claim whenever he took his shirt off, and the knowledge of such excited him and his wolf.

Reaching out, he pushed a stray lock of her hair behind her ear. Her eyes opened. She rolled toward him before placing her hand over the mark on his chest. The nearness of her lithe body allowed her scent to wrap around them.

"Good morning." The husky quality of her voice shot straight to his balls.

"Morning." Chris shifted their position so she was under him. "Did you sleep well?" He adjusted her leg over his hip.

"I did." She sighed. "Like a baby."

"So did I."

Positioned at her entrance, he pushed forward, easing into her snug pussy. The warm, silky heat wrapped around him, encasing him in liquid heaven. *Goddamn, she's perfect.* She rippled around him, opening up to his intrusion. Her soft gasps were an aphrodisiac, heating his blood. Along with the way she dug her fingers into his shoulders.

Lily scored her nails down his back then settled her palms on his ass, pushing him deeper inside her. She draped her other leg over his, changing the angle of his penetration.

"Best way to start the day." He growled, his pace still relaxed, unhurried.

Lily smiled and gave a small laugh. The inner muscles of her sex clenched and unclenched, sending pulses of agonizing pleasure through him. "Yes, it is."

Lowering his head, Chris took her nipple into his mouth. He scored the sensitive bead with his teeth then bit down. She shivered with a whimper. He did it again, this time to the other bud. He reached up to cup her breast, kneading the supple flesh before pinching her hardened nipple.

He wanted to see her reaction to a bit of pain. Her pussy went slick. Her breath hitched. He smirked to himself. His dick jerked at the idea of her wearing his clamps as he fucked her. "You like a bit of pain with your pleasure, she-wolf." He nuzzled her neck.

"I-I don't know."

He pinched her nipple again, holding it for the count of five. Lily squealed, bucking against him while her head thrashed from side to side.

"Take it, she-wolf. Take it for your mate." His pace quickened. The heady way she responded to him had him holding onto his control by a fine thread.

A thin sheen of perspiration covered her skin. Her cry of pleasure excited him, motivated his next plan of action. Without warning, he rolled them over, and guided her over him.

They rocked together, climbing toward their mutual satisfaction. Chris cupped her breasts, squeezing and tugging on them. "Chris...." she cried.

"Take me with you, she-wolf." He groaned. Her changing pace kept him on edge and brought him closer to his release than he'd been prepared for.

He ground up into her, rubbing his groin against her clit, which also shortened her strokes, adding a new dimension to her movement. Her breath came in soft pants as her hand curled into a fist.

When she leaned back, her hard nub peeked out from its protective hood, and his mouth watered. Later, he'd taste her there. Later, he'd make her sweet pussy a feast. Swiping his finger over the hard bundle of nerves, she cried out. He did it again while meeting her thrust for thrust. Fire raced down his spine and settled in his balls. Yet, he held out a little more.

She tensed over him, and, at exact second, he pulled her down to him and marked her again. Her pleasured scream sent him over the edge with her. He thrust twice more then gave a low moan, spilling his seed deep inside her.

*\*\**

"Are you hungry?" He poured some juice then brought the glass to his lips.

"Famished." She leaned against the counter next to him and smiled.

When they were able to move last night, Chris carried her into his bathroom and ran the shower for them. "Vanilla" was nice with Lily, but he still needed more. The way she accepted his touch let him know she might be receptive to the plan he'd enact soon.

"How about we grab a burger at the diner?"

"I'd like that."

"Great." He finished his drink then placed the empty glass in the kitchen sink. Holding his hand out, he waited for her to take it.

Lily placed her palm in his. "I should have thought to bring a change of clothes."

Last night, when they arrived at home and after he'd put her to bed, he'd picked up their discarded clothes. He liked her simple little dress. It fit her personality. "Well, it's not like you wore it very long." He waggled his brows at her.

A pretty pink blush suffused her cheeks. "This is true. You just got me worked up."

"You did the same to me. You pushed all my buttons with your sassy mouth." He led her to the truck before opening the door for her. "Plus you smelled so good, I had to have you."

Again, the soft, subtle scent of her arousal wrapped around him.

She glanced up at him. "You smell really good, too."

"Do I?"

She nodded. "Wild with an undertone of leather."

Chris pulled her to him and kissed her. He showed her with his mouth just how much she affected him with only the sugary aroma of her pussy. He slipped his hand under her dress and hissed when he came in contact with skin only.

She gave him a coy smile as he stepped back. "I couldn't find them."

The thought of spending lunch with Lily, sitting at a table with her not wearing any panties, drove him insane. "Are you trying to get yourself fucked again?"

"Maybe." She climbed into the vehicle. Her indirect challenge awakened the other beast. The one who craved her submission. The one who wanted to see her kneeling before him.

*Soon,* he reminded himself. He had to put everything out there first. He had to tell her the truth about himself. Though mating hadn't necessary been the plan for last night, it happened and he didn't regret it. He'd discovered she liked a bit of pain, but what else?

The idea of restraining her, ass up in the air for his pleasure, fanned the flames of the heated ardor building in him. He got in beside her, and started the truck, the whole time making a mental checklist of the things he'd love to do with her and to her.

The special space in his house he told her about housed his toys. Though it didn't necessarily double as a playroom, if he wanted to experiment in there, he could. But, he had a feeling he'd need more room when it came to their play.

"What do I tell my family?" Her voice cut through the mental images of the different scenes he'd like to act out with her.

"You're mated?"

Her fingers twisted in the hem of the dress. "Yeah, seems simple enough."

"Are you worried what they'd say about it?" He knew being the youngest of the Truesdale children came with its own set of challenges.

"I don't know. I feel a little awkward about it. They'll sense exactly what we were doing."

Chris laughed. He knew he shouldn't have. "Do you think your brothers feel awkward when they see you after fucking their respective mates?"

She seemed to consider his question then shook her head. "No, probably not."

"So why should you be worried?"

"It's different. I can't explain it, but it is."

Chris pulled onto the main road heading for Gee's bar. "Yes, in a way, I suppose it is. However, your life is your life. What we do in our home is our business. Not theirs."

"I guess you're right. It's all so new and different."

"It is for me, too, she-wolf. Which brings me to what I wanted to talk to you about last night." Better to broach the subject now before they entered the diner than while they sat there. Definitely didn't need a repeat of what happened the night before.

"Okay."

"There are certain things about me," he hedged. "My appetite runs a little darker than most."

Lily stared at him. Her curious gaze lit with a bit of apprehension. "Darker?"

"Yes. You see, I expect things from...women."

"Does this have to do with the Dungeon?" The uneasy edge in her voice had him second-guessing himself. Yet, since he'd already started, he had to finish.

"Yes. The Dungeon is a BDSM club. Do you know what kind of place it is?" If she did, it would surprise the hell out of him.

"A club where you pick up women?" Her sudden change in tune had been a metaphorical splash of cold water in his face.

"Not necessarily. I'm a Dominant."

"Well, duh." She relaxed into the leather seat of his truck. "I know."

Chris quirked a brow. "I think you're missing something. Last night, when I pinched your nipple until you cried out? I craved the bite of pain from you."

Lily frowned. "You want to hurt me?"

"Yes, but not in the most conventional way." He pondered how to explain this little tidbit about himself without freaking her out. "I like submissive women."

"I'm not an omega."

No, she was a beta, through and through. "I know. It's not the same type of submissive. I crave a sexual submissive."

Recognition blazed in her eyes. "You want to be in charge in the bedroom."

"Yes." He breathed a sigh of relief when she didn't try to jump from the truck.

"Like how?"

"I'm partial to bondage, but I do like some impact play." To him, being a Dom was like her being a rancher, it was just who he was.

"Impact," she repeated. "Spanking, right?"

"Uh-huh." He waited for her to blow a gasket and call him all kinds of depraved names.

"What's the bondage part?"

"Tie you up." He leaned closer and growled. "Have my wicked way with you while you scream and beg me to let you come."

Lily's nostrils flared. Her pulse kicked up a notch. "You were going to tell me this last night."

"All of it."

"So those women who you...."

"Subs. Both of us were getting our own gratification from our meeting." Truth. He kept his play as impersonal as he could. Yes, he had sex, but it had been a function with them, a way to gain a natural high from a freely given power exchange.

"Will you be taking me there?"

He took a moment, trying to gauge her reception to the idea. Did it repulse her? Testing the air between them, he scented no jealousy or anger, only an innocent inquisitiveness and some excitement. His wolf sat up, watching her with keen interest. "When you're ready, if you want."

"So how's this all supposed to play out?"

"Well, first, we're going to go in and have something to eat then we're going to go home, and I want you to think about what I told you. In two days, we'll revisit this conversation and you can tell me your answer."

A tinge of disappointment tamped down the arousal in her natural perfume. This had been why he'd wanted to mate her after he explained everything. Unfortunately, sometimes a wolf had to do what a wolf had to do.

"Lead the way." Lily eased out of the truck.

*Fuck.*

# Chapter Ten

"Burger, please." She gifted Paul with a grin as she sat down at the bar. Things had been a little tense between her and Chris since his instructions the day before, and she needed a little sister time with Fawn. She hoped a burger bribe would be enough to get help figuring out what to do next. "How's PG doing?"

After placing her order where Gee could see it, Paul began to write out his answer. She stilled his hand. Then signed. *I'm learning. Go slow.*

Paul smiled and began moving his hands. *She's great. Happy. Be here later.*

*Great!* They talked for a minute more until Gee called him over to take another order.

*Popular man's work's never done.* He laughed.

The full-bodied sound warmed her. *Later, Paul.*

He nodded. *Congratulations on your mating.* He motioned to her neck. *Best thing in the whole world.*

She grinned then mouthed, *thank you.*

"Don't be hitting on my wait staff." Gee's gruff tone cut through the idle chatter floating on the air.

"I'm not."

"Good." He regarded her for another minute. "Chris treating you well?"

"Miss Fern or Miss Lonnie fix you up with a little omega of your own yet?" She arched a brow.

He scrunched up his face and grumbled, "No." He blew out a breath. "Won't neither."

The massive logs he called arms were crossed, and a stern look graced his face. Narrowed whiskey-colored eyes assessed her. *Intimidation, thy name is Gee.* Lily grinned then glanced back at the door. She loved teasing the old bear, sometimes more than she should. He stood over her for a minute longer before someone called out to him and he strolled away.

"Hey, what are you doing over here all alone?" Hannah's voice surprised her.

"Grabbing lunch. What brings you here?"

"Well, I may have heard you might be here." She sat down beside Lily. "So, is it true? Did you mate him?"

*How in the world?* Wait, no, she knew. The town liked to gossip, especially with the rebirth of the pack. "I wear his mark."

Her friend's face lit up. "Congratulations."

"Thanks."

"You don't seem happy about it." Hannah laid her hand over Lily's.

"No, I am. He's given me some things to think over."

"Shouldn't he have brought those up beforehand?"

Heat suffused her cheeks. "Um, you see, I kind of—"

"Say no more." She laughed. "Mates have a way

of doing things."

"Yes." She chuckled.

"When are you guys supposed to talk about it again?"

"Tomorrow night. He wants me completely sure about us and what I want. We're doing this completely backwards."

"It happens."

"Sure." She shrugged. "So, how're Micha and Jessie?"

"They're great. Jessie has been talking nonstop about Jordan and his promise." Hannah grinned. "The girl is a trickster through and through. She's got incredible negotiating skills. I swear she'll grow up to be a lawyer."

"I'll talk with Tinks and see if Jordan can come over sometime next week."

"Don't worry about it," Hannah replied. "You have more important things to concern yourself with than their playdates. When everything has settled for you and Chris then we'll work on it."

Lily nodded. "Sounds great." Paul reappeared a few seconds later and handed her a bag. *You're a lifesaver.* "I'll see you later, Hannah." Lily waved as she headed for the door.

Once she left Chris's house, she'd wanted to go home and think, maybe breathe without his hovering. No, she wasn't being fair. He meant well, and she'd been on the quiet side, too, holding everything in. Instead, she went for a run to clear her head and think things through. But every time she tried to make sense of it all, everything got muddled again. Eventually, she picked a spot by the stream near the pastureland and rested. When she got home, the house was empty. She showered and dressed in some clothes she'd left behind, just in case, then made the trek to town. Seeing as Kal and Graham would be out working the fields and with the cows, now seemed like the perfect time to talk to Fawn, hence the burger.

She started the long hike home...or what used to be home. The cool air invigorated her, and the walk gave her a chance to think things through. She'd always known Chris was different. Always knew he could be an asshole when something didn't go his way. However, she never expected him to say, "Hey, by the way, I'm a Dom."

How did one become such? What made him want to do those things and what did it say about the women who accepted it? Since Roland had boosted Internet and cell signals, she figured once she told Fawn everything, she'd go surfing—or whatever humans called it.

She stood on the front porch of her home and stared at the door. The plain weathered white door was simple. Yet, all but a few of her memories were ingrained in those four walls behind an old, worn door. She entered. "Hello, anyone home?"

She placed the bag on the kitchen table. *Go figure. The one day I need to talk to someone, everyone is gone.* "Fawn?"

The soft rumbling of voices caught her attention, and she followed them down the hall to the office Fawn used for her business—which she also used to manage the ranch. Lily thought she'd be mad at the change. Instead, she felt the weight of the world being lifted from her shoulders. Between taking care of the house and managing the book side of the family farm, most days overwhelmed her.

Whatever program Fawn used for her accounting business, she implemented it for their cattle. It took three-quarters of the work away from what Lily had been doing by hand.

"So, if I add ice cream to the cafe, what will my profit margin be?" Ero's, owner of Los Lobos Cafe, voice filled the hallway.

"I'm not sure. As you know Dotties is open and we still have The Den, I would wait a bit before you decide to go this route. Remember, you not only have to buy the counter to hold the ice cream, but you also need the freezer to keep it," Fawn answered.

He grunted. "What are my profits now?"

"You're actually doing good...."

Lily made her way back to the kitchen. She didn't need to hear about Ero's business, nor did she want to interfere. When the six foot four inch wolf with blue eyes and black hair emerged from Fawn's office, she waved.

"Hey, stranger." He smiled. "Haven't seen you in a while."

"Likewise. How are you?"

"Good." He pointed back to where Fawn sat in the other room. "Business."

She nodded. "Everything going good for you and your brother?" Known as the light and dark twins. Where Ero had dark hair and light eyes, his brother had sandy-blond hair, hazel eyes, and he was a pack protector. Both were enigmas. Both were still single in a pack which seemed to be pairing up at a rather rapid pace.

"We're good. Busy as all get out." He glanced at his phone. "I'll see you around."

Taken aback by the sudden dismissal, she watched Ero's retreating form as he stepped into the mudroom before exiting the house.

"You're home." Fawn waddled out to the kitchen. "Did you ha— *Holy shit!*"

Lily winced. "Surprise?"

Fawn laughed and sat down across from her. "Not in the least." She pointed to the bag. "Did you bring me a burger from Gee's?"

She nodded.

"I love you. I'm famished." Fawn grabbed the sack. "Did you know it would happen?"

"It" being her mating Chris. "No. Well, I should have known. Everything is up in the air still."

Fawn arched a brow. "So you're bribing me with a burger to help you?"

"More like helping me figure out what the heck I've gotten myself into with him." She blew out an exasperated breath. "I didn't know being a mate came with subsections."

Her mated sister blinked. "What?"

"Chris wants me to try things with him. Tie me up. Spank me." Her cheeks grew increasingly warmer as she ticked off the things she and he talked about.

"O-kay. Well, I guess you need to ask yourself if this is what you really want. You can't take back the mating. It's true and complete. However, everything else is both of your choices. He lets you know what he wants. The question becomes can you handle it? Is it what you want?"

Lily nodded as Fawn took a bite of the burger and moaned. Did she really want what Chris offered? She couldn't lie, the things he'd said he'd done added an extra bit of titillation to the mating. The things he expressed to her also intrigued her.

"I believe I have something to think about." She sighed. "Who's cooking tonight?"

Her mated sister shrugged. "Might end up going out again."

"Why?"

"Have you ever eaten your brother's cooking?"

Lily laughed. "You've got a point there. How about I cook you guys a few meals for the next couple of days, and, as payment, you can tell me the names you've come up with for the baby."

"Deal."

\*\*\*

Sitting in the office, Lily opened her laptop and pulled up her favorite search engine. Her fingers hovered over the keys, anticipating her next move. Four simple letters and a word. So, why couldn't she type it in? Nervous energy wiggled through her stomach. She licked her bottom lip and closed her eyes. *What the hell are you waiting for?*

She typed it in then hit enter. Several sites along with videos popped up in front of her. She chose the easy stuff first—a beginner's site, a guide of sorts. She clicked on the link and waited as the page opened. Inch by inch more of the page appeared. *Welcome to Kink 101....*

Black-and-white piping framed a letter introducing the owners of the blog. The woman, named Scarlet Kitty, wrote about her life as a service submissive. Twenty-four hours a day, seven days a week. Pictures accompanied her testimony. In most she was naked, others she wore skimpy, barely there clothing. She wore a thick, black dog collar with a ring jutting out from the front of it.

Another picture had a man, balding, in his mid-forties, standing behind her. He wore a white button-down shirt, leather pants, and leather gloves. She looked up adoringly into his eyes, and he had the softest smile Lily had ever seen. The caption stated she called him Sir, and they'd been partners for twenty-six years. Strange titles humans gave their mates. Partners, spouses. Lovers, friends with benefits. Lily rolled her eyes at that one. The newest one, before she returned to the hills, had been called *Netflix and Chill*. Why couldn't humans be more like wolves? Find their mates, claim them, and be happy?

She pushed the wayward thoughts away, knowing she'd only distract herself from the task of learning all she could. The letter concluded a few sentences later with *Thank you for stopping by. If you have any questions, email us at....* No, she'd definitely not be emailing anyone. Instead, she hovered the arrow over the sections of the site. Bondage. Impact. Fetishes. One even said, *Puppy Play. Humans are so curious.*

Although she'd spent several years with them and learned some human customs, they'd stayed to themselves when they could. Her mom and dad worked themselves to the bone to support all three—not as if her brothers slacked off. Kal and Graham had done their best then took over when her parents died.

Lily shook off the memories of her parents' death. They were gone. Her mom and dad wouldn't want her to dwell on the loss or the achingly huge hole it left in her heart when they died. They wanted her to be happy and for the most part she had been.

"Lily?" Kal opened the door to the office. "Fawn said you'd come home. Is everything okay?"

She closed the lid of her laptop and brushed the stray tears from her eyes. She didn't need some damn Web site to tell her how to act or what to do or even what was expected of her. Her mate would guide her, teach her anything she desired to know, as long as she opened up to him and gave him the same respect in return.

"I'm fine. I brought Fawn some lunch and I promised to cook dinner, too." She stood from where she sat then came around the desk and hugged her brother.

"He treating you okay?"

"Chris is fine. He didn't hurt me or anything. He was...is really good to me. He's giving me time to reconcile our lives together."

"So you went and did it, huh?" Kal whispered, pushing her hair behind her ear.

"I did." She grinned. "I'm spreading my wings and leaving the nest."

He sighed. The hair on the top of her head fluttered. "This will always be your home. Don't you forget it."

"I won't."

# Chapter Eleven

At seven p.m., a knock came at Chris's door. The idea of Lily never coming back, though the mating bond tied them together, had sprung to his mind a couple of times.

In fact, he'd decided to tell her never mind. Then reneged. She deserved all of her mate as he demanded all of her. He strode to the door, no expectations for what would come. He pulled it open, and the breath he'd been holding left him with a whoosh. "Lily." He gathered her in his arms and held her tight.

Giving her time to think, he realized, had been a horrible, horrible idea.

"Wow, is this going to be how you greet me every time I come home?" She nuzzled his neck and drew in a breath.

"I'd be lying if I didn't say I was a little worried." He ushered her inside and closed them in.

"Wait." She placed her hand against his chest. "The rest of my stuff is on the porch." She stepped outside to grab her things. "Do you have someplace I can put these?"

"Yes," he answered, almost too quickly for his taste.

"Great. How about you show me where then I'll make us some dinner." She shimmied past him.

He snatched her arm and twirled her back around. "What?"

She grinned up at him, her slate-blue eyes twinkling with mirth. The pulse at her throat throbbed to the beat of her heart. His wolf pushed forward at her soft inhalation. "Dinner. I'll make it."

The subtle fragrance of her arousal wafted around him, teasing him. Tempting the beast within him. "Just like that?"

"Were you expecting me to put up a fight?"

*Yes.* When he'd dropped his proclamation of having her spend a couple of nights away from him, he'd thought she'd pitch a fit and make him pay for even suggesting so. "Kind of."

She nodded. "Fair enough. I thought about it. I even did a little research. I think subconsciously I searched for something bad."

The idea of her looking up the terms, finding out what turned her on, or what repulsed her, had his cock thickening in his jeans. "What did you find?"

"A couple in love." She strode down the hall, a sway to her hips while her curly brown hair brushed across her shoulders with each step.

"What?" He followed behind her, curious as to what she'd found.

"Yes." She pointed to the dresser he'd placed near his. "Mine?"

"Yeah."

"Great. I'll put this stuff away. Why don't you

take something out for me to make dinner?"

His cheeks heated. The only food he'd bought came in a to-go box from one of the local establishments. "Yeah we might have a problem there."

"Why?" She opened her bag before carrying some shirts and things to the dresser. On the way back, she pushed her hair behind her ear.

"Well, I don't usually keep food on hand. People, for the most part, feed me." He rubbed the back of his neck. "I usually eat on my 'late in the day calls.' It's something the wives of my clients insist on."

"Well, we can grab something, then." She carried another armful of clothes to the dresser.

"Stop," he barked. The harshness of his tone had been harder than he'd intended.

"Did I do something wrong?" She sat on the bed next to her bags.

"No. You've come in here like a tornado, stamping your place in our home while also saying you read about a couple." He had questions to ask. Things to say.

"Then I'll finish up here, and we'll be ready to go. Or you could order us something from the pizza place in Hill City. Gabby and I go there when we see Alicia."

"Pizza?"

"Fully loaded. Meat, extra cheese, veggies. So good. You'll love it. We can kick up our feet, chat about everything."

He stared at her for a minute. "You'll tell me what you found in your research?"

"Yes."

"Fine, go call and I'll get the rest of this settled

for us." He moved toward her bag as she stood. "We'll discuss what happens later while we eat."

She gave him a curt nod before exiting the room. Chris moved to the closet and grabbed the items, including something he'd picked up for her while in Rapid City for a call. The lacy outfit would fit her like a glove and make her eye color pop.

He placed the things on the bed, her side then finished putting everything away, while adding her toiletries to the bathroom. Already the house felt like a home. Not just some place he'd lay his head. In a moment's time, every ill feeling he had, every worry seemed to melt away. Old wounds healed.

"Pizza's ordered," Lily called from down the hall.

"I'll be right there."

Placing the last of her belongings in the drawers, he closed them then stored her bags in the closet. He went to the living room and found Lily by the door waiting for him. She stared out at the starry night, her arms crossed. Her bottom lip between her teeth.

Her features were soft. A few freckles dappled her delicate jaw. Her button nose and full lips were showcased by beautiful eyes, and he swore her eyelashes were a mile long. They fluttered shut seconds before she gifted him a brilliant smile.

*Mate.*

"Ready to go?" He grabbed his keys off the cork board while strolling toward her.

"Ready," she answered, holding out her hand.

\*\*\*

Two pieces of pizza in, she couldn't stand it any longer. The almost-silent treatment they'd been giving each other grated on her nerves. How the hell were they supposed to go forward when he wouldn't tell her a damn thing?

Lily glanced at Chris who grabbed another slice of pizza from the box. Unlike her, he appeared relaxed, almost copacetic with their arrangement. She wanted to scream. Tell him to hurry up and eat the damn pizza and move on. Rather, she sat there, staring off into space, trying to calm the erratic emotions coursing through her.

"You're awful quiet over there." He took another bite.

"What do you want me to say?"

"Why don't you tell me about the couple you read about?"

"I went looking for more information after I left here this afternoon."

"I'm glad you did your research." The hint of approval in his voice warmed her.

"I thought if I was going to walk into this with both eyes open, I should know what BDSM is and if it'll work for me. Let me tell you, there are some crazy sites out there."

Chris laughed. "Yes, there are. What did you find?"

"A site called Kink 101 and a woman named Scarlet Kitty. Anyway, her opening letter caught my attention. There were pictures of her and a man by the name of Sir." She recounted the whole site, from each drop-down menu to the stories added in by other couples.

"How did it make you feel?"

"Intrigued. I liked the idea of being tied up. I liked the idea, I guess, of being spanked. But, I don't like the extreme side of it. All those...torture devices. All the...misery. I know they enjoy it. Not me. I'd hate it."

He nodded. "Then we'll keep it light. Doesn't have to go to the extreme side of play. Besides, it's not the kind of Dom I am."

"I need a safe word. Right?"

"Yes. Something not in your normal vocabulary. Something you wouldn't scream out during sex."

"Magnum." Even annunciating his name left a sour taste in her mouth.

"A little severe, don't you think?"

She shrugged. "It works. We both know I won't ever use his name."

"I don't like it." Chris curled his lip. "Yes, it's not a word you'd say, ever. Still, I won't have the bastard's name uttered if we got to a point of needing it. We'll go with red."

She learned the color scale while researching, never thinking she could choose the word as her own. *I still have so much to learn.* "Fine. Red. I'll use it." She knew if she ever uttered it, he'd immediately stop what they were doing. Which, she liked. The other colors were just as simple. Yellow to pause, if things got too intense, and green meant she was enjoying herself—didn't want what they were doing to stop.

"Good," he stated. "In our room are some items. I want you to examine them, and, if you're willing to accept this new dynamic of our relationship, I want you to change into the outfit I picked up for you. Then I'd like you to join me back in here in fifteen minutes."

She sat there for a moment and considered him and his offer. How had she missed this? Missed the outfit and the objects he bought. Everything seemed like one big secret. The answers came with each step she took. She leaned in and pressed a kiss to his lips then stood. The final test in her mind, if their mating would be a true, full mating, where each of them could accept each other for their quirks. Or if they were going to have half a mating, where Chris hid this part of himself because she couldn't approve of him.

On the pillow on the left side of his bed sat a bundle of rope, some kind of clamps with chain, a lacy nightie, and a calico-print bandanna. She studied each item. Her fingers brushed over the soft, almost parachute-type cord, and the powder-blue handkerchief. She studied the lacy details of the blush-colored nightie. Simple yet elegant. *Is this how he sees me?* Simple and elegant? Testing the strength of the clamps, a niggle of pleasure bloomed in her belly. From the pictures she'd seen, she knew the devices would be attached to her nipples, and after their night in the woods, she enjoyed the bit of pain Chris administrated.

After placing the clamps on the bed, her decision made, she took off her clothes to prepare for the evening, resolute in her choice. Her hands didn't tremble like she thought they would. Determination filled her while she slipped the skimpy piece of material over her body. With the rest of the stuff Chris left for her in her hands, she made her way out to the living room. What she saw when she arrived, took her breath away.

Chris stood by the fireplace. Naked from the waist up, the muscles of his broad back bunched when he turned toward her. The pure unadulterated lust in his gaze took her breath away. "Let's begin."

# Chapter Twelve

*Fuck.* The nightie clung to her curves like a second skin. Her strawberry-colored nipples beaded under his inspection, and his mouth watered. A tempting little morsel all for him. She stood in the entryway, clutching the toys he'd bought for her.

"Stand before me." The wolf crawled to the surface.

The sass he loved so much about his she-wolf presented itself as she stepped forward. Her coy smirk, and the flutter of her lashes only added to the heady game she played with him. "Should I kneel?" Her husky tone shot straight to his groin.

"I see you learned protocol, too." He took the bundle of rope from her hands. "Turn around and put your hands behind your back."

Heat blazed in her slate-blue eyes as she turned to give him her back. The long straight line of her spine drew his attention down to her round, firm ass, and the cute little dimples at the base of her back. He'd picked the perfect berry tint for her. It enhanced her creamy flesh. She placed the bandanna and clamps on the table in front of her.

"Here's how this will work." He unfurled the rope then grabbed both ends to draw it together. "I'm going to tie your arms first."

The pulse at her neck increased. "Okay."

"We're not doing formalities tonight." He skimmed his fingers down her arms before drawing them together. "So relax." He began winding the rope around her wrists first then up her forearms. "Later, when you're more comfortable with what we're doing, you'll call me, Sir."

Lily nodded. "I understand."

With each knot he tied, her chest jutted outward a bit more. He wove the rope into an intricate design, one meant to keep her arms immobile and sweeten her submission. When he finished, he stepped around her. "Comfortable?" He drew his knuckle over her already-hard nipple and enjoyed her slight shudder.

"It's different." She licked her lips. "Confining, but I like it." She rolled her shoulders, prior to tugging at her arms.

"Good to know. Ready for the next step?"

"Yes."

Chris plucked the bandanna up from the table. He rolled it into a blindfold big enough to cover her eyes. The idea had occurred to him a couple of times over the last few days he should have grabbed a sleeping mask. But he liked throwing in bits of the country girl flare he'd grown to love all those years ago.

Once more, he stood behind her and lifted the blindfold into place. Her lips parted and a small gasp caught his attention while he finished tying the knot.

"Can you see anything?"

"No." Her breathy tone sent a surge of adrenaline through his body.

"Now, the final step." He picked up the clamps next and waited. Testing the resistance of the clamps, he studied her. How long could he stand there before she'd say something or call out for him?

The sweet tendrils of her desire wrapped around him. He scented no fear or anxiety. If anything, her impatience flowed along with her need. He watched the bob of her throat as she swallowed before licking her lips.

Running his finger between her breasts, he traced her curves. Her soft moan had his dick thickening even more. "This won't do," he murmured. "You're way too overdressed."

"I-I can't take it off," she muttered, pressing into his touch.

"Don't you worry about a thing." He guided her toward the couch. "I've got you covered." He sat down then pulled her between his legs and groaned. She was at the perfect height for him to suck on her pretty little tits.

He eased the thin straps over her shoulders and allowed the flimsy material to drift down her body. Her high, pert breasts tempted him. His mouth watered as the beads puckered under his perusal. The pretty blush-colored nipples called to him.

Leaning into her, Chris swiped his tongue over the peak. He nipped at the nub. Sucked it. The soft mewling sounds she made were music to his ears. She loved nipple play. He drew on the bud, sucking it with hard, even pulls. Releasing it, Chris placed the clamp on it.

Lily screamed. She wiggled in his arms while gritting her teeth. "Too much. It hurts. It hurts."

"Shhh," he crooned, trying to soothe her. "You can take it for me. Breathe. In...out."

She took several deep breaths before settling. "Oh wow, it's different now."

Chris flicked the end with his finger. "Are you ready for the other?"

"Yes."

"Such a brave girl." He brushed his lips over hers. He kissed a path across her jaw onto her neck, stopping momentarily at the mating mark. He laved the damaged section of flesh, tonguing it. She panted, leaning into him as she swayed.

Chris steadied her, holding her in place with one hand as he administered the same treatment to the neglected breast. When he clamped it, she sucked in air but followed the same breathing exercise. He gave a quick tug and watched her go to the balls of her feet, placing all of her weight on his shoulder.

Her cries of pleasure filled the living room along with the crack of Chris smacking her ass.

She stilled. "You hit me."

A chuckle rumbled in his chest. "I did." He smacked the other cheek. "I like knowing you'll wear all my marks."

Her heartbeat ratcheted up another notch.

"But we'll save a more intimate spanking for another time. Right now, I need inside you." As it was, his dick throbbed behind the confines of his jeans and feeling her hair brush his chest, only made it worse. After helping Lily stand, he shucked his jeans before directing her over his lap.

Her sugary pussy dripped with cream, searing

his skin. He ran a finger through her folds then brought it to his mouth and sucked the wetness from it. "So fucking good. Like honey. Ease up a little bit, she-wolf."

She sat up, giving him room to position himself at her entrance. Lily lowered herself onto his dick and took him in one stroke. Her tight channel rippled around him, accommodating his size. "Chris," she whimpered.

"I got you." He rubbed her clit with his thumb. "Get off on me. Come, so I can fuck you hard."

Her hips undulated, rocking at an uneven pace. With each swipe of his thumb, she bucked until she rode him hard, lifting up and down on him before grinding against his groin. He let out a low groan as she came hard. Her release threatened to unman him, but he wasn't even close to being done with her.

Her cries turned to soft pants while she nuzzled his neck. Chris set them at a steady pace, intermittently pulling on the chain connecting the clamps. He swore she grew tighter with each tug, and fuck if it didn't feel good. Way too good. He couldn't stop the need to come. Fire raced up and down his spine while he tried to hold back the inevitable. "Fuck."

"Yes," she cried. "I need...please."

"So good." He rolled her clit between his fingers. "Let go, Lily, and take me with you."

His pace quickened, becoming erratic with each pump of his hips. The sounds emanating from both of them were an erotic song of two mates finding their pleasure in one another.

Chris buried his face in her neck and licked the mark before latching onto her skin and biting down.

The world narrowed down to him and her. Their cries of completion rang out as she rode him through the waves of her release, which drew out his climax. Her body went limp in his arms as he held her to him. "You're amazing, she-wolf."

"You're not so bad yourself."

\*\*\*

*Hill City*

Lily hurried around Alicia's place, trying to set up the last of the party favors and treats. The men were out in the small detached garage, enjoying a beer and watching some ball game with Poppa and Hombre. Hannah and Violet, a wolf Miss Fern sent to help Gabby, and Fawn were already there, helping out as well.

The front door opened again, and Elle came inside. "I'm here."

Graham backed out of the house. "And I'm leaving. Where are the guys?"

"In the garage," Fawn called out. "They're watching a game."

"I swear they're afraid of what will happen to them if they have fun with women." Violet rolled her eyes.

Gabby laughed and rubbed her growing belly. "I think they know and it really does scare the shit out of them."

The little raven-haired mouse of a girl blushed. "I only meant—"

"She knows, child," Miss Fern announced walking into the room. "She was messing with you." Lily's mated mother narrowed her eyes at Gabby. "Be

93

good, girl."

"Is there room for one more?" Ginger called out, pushing into the house. "Where did the men go?"

"Out back," Miss Claire answered. "They're gathered around a television watching men in uniforms smack a ball around. I have never in my entire life seen anything so silly."

"Has anyone seen Alicia yet?" Gabby grabbed a carrot slice off the platter nearest her.

"Not yet. She said she had one more place she needed to stop before she'd be home. If we have to start without her, go ahead."

Gabby nodded. "Sounds like her. She's been out of her mind busy. Add in these two"—she pointed to her belly—"and she's been frazzled."

A knock came at the door again then Brienne entered the house. The willowy therapist grinned. "I heard we were having a babies party. I couldn't miss it." She made a circuit around the space, hugging everyone. Her warm energy invigorated everyone.

"Where's Shawn?" Lily asked.

"Oh, he saw Graham and headed to the garage." She laughed.

"Do you think we should bring them food?" Gabby frowned at the table set up for them.

"Hush." Miss Fern nudged her. "Henry has stuff out there for them."

"Well, let's get this show on the road." Lily clapped her hands together. "We have games and presents and all kinds of stuff."

At the last minute, their alpha, Drew, and his mate, Betty, strolled into the house. "We're not late, are we?" His deep resonating voice captured all of their attention. Since he'd killed Magnum, Drew had worked tirelessly to make sure the pack prospered where it had deteriorated before his return.

"Of course not!" Gabby ushered them into the house. "But the guys are watching a ball game out in the garage if you'd rather be there."

"Don't mind if I do." He grinned. "Congratulations, ladies."

Once he left, the party started. They played games, opened presents, and had fun. So far, the idea had been a success. Having the party at Poppa's and Alicia's turned out to be a good idea. Even though Alicia hadn't come home yet.

Gabby had stared at the door a few times, but never said a word. Yes, it worried all of them, but sometimes, getting from the hills to Rapid City could be tricky. They all blamed it on traffic or her having more to do than she planned.

When the men joined them, they all assured the girls nothing was wrong and everything would work out the way it should. The day hadn't been ruined, in fact, it had been one of the best days for her growing family. Fawn and Gabby had enough clothes to outfit a small army, and the other odds and ends they had would keep their babies busy for a long time.

As the sun slipped below the horizon, they waved good-bye to the last of the guests. A niggle of worry filled her stomach as a highway patrol car pulled into the driveway. *Oh no.* Her bottom lip trembled. The inexplicable feeling of sadness washed over her as a black car pulled in behind the SDHP vehicle.

A man got out of the first car while two more got out of the second. The man in front donned his hat then gazed at the gathered group waiting outside. "I'm looking for Ernesto Cruz."

Poppa stepped forward. Confusion filled his features. "I'm Ernesto."

Sadness rolled off the man in sickening waves. She wanted to howl in outrage. *No. No. No. No.*

"Could you come with me, please? I'm afraid I have some horrible news." He held his hand out to Poppa.

The older man began to crumple, and Black Jack and Hombre were there to catch him. "Please God not my baby. Not my Alicia."

Lily buried her face in Chris's chest, unable to take the scene playing out in front of her. What started out as a happy day became a bitter pill she didn't think anyone could swallow. The front door of the house banged open, and Lily glanced up. Gabby stood on the porch, Kru right behind her.

"What's going on? What happened?" She ambled down the stairs as best she could, Kru holding onto her the whole time.

"I'm sorry, miss." The patrolman frowned. "There's been a terrible accident. Alicia Cruz has passed away."

Gabby screamed. Oh God, for the rest of her life, Lily would remember the sound her mated sister made. Kru picked her up and carried her back inside while Black Jack and Hombre helped Poppa to the car then hurried to their bikes.

Lily didn't know what to do. "Easy, angel. We'll stay with her. She's our family."

Kalum and Fawn voiced the same sentiments as they walked toward the house. The deep throb of the motorcycles filled the still night air then disappeared down the road, following the Highway Patrol.

"We should call Bas." Gabby would need him.

Just in case. She wiped the tears from her eyes. "We need to let everyone know." She went into work mode. She had to keep her mind occupied.

"Good idea." Chris rubbed her arms then stepped away.

She could hear Gabby's cries from the room down the hall, and she finally let loose a mournful howl. Three more joined her.

\*\*\*

A week later, they stood in the same spot they'd been in when the state police showed up. Alicia's funeral had been perfect. They'd laughed and cried...mostly cried. Gabby sat huddled with her mate. Bastian, the pack doctor, with the help of Caress, one of the pack healers, had given her a couple of herbal sedatives she could take without worrying about hurting her babies.

Poppa was...inconsolable. As soon as they arrived back at the house, he holed up in his room. Brie had offered her services, but he didn't even appear to understand what she offered. Instead, he grabbed a full bottle of Jack Daniels and took off. Lily didn't blame the man. The love of his life was gone.

She glanced up at Chris who held onto her. "What do we do?"

"What we always do. Help." He kissed the top of her head. "Come on, it's getting dark."

She nodded and followed him to the truck. "I don't like them being alone."

"Kru and Gabby are going to stay for a few days. If they need anything, they'll call." He brushed her nose with his before closing the door and rounding the hood. When he got in, he grasped her hand. "We'll get them through this. I promise."

"I know." She stared up at the house as he backed out of the driveway. "I need you to understand how much I love you."

Nothing like death to make her realize, even though they were wolves and would live long, full lives, it could affect them so profoundly.

He gave her a cocky yet somber grin. "I promise, for the rest of my life, I will tell you every day, how much I love you, too, she-wolf."

"Let's go home."

# About the Author

TL Reeve, was born out of a love of family and a bond that became unbreakable. Living in Alabama, TL misses Los Angeles, and will one day return to the beaches of Southern California to ride the waves at Huntington Beach. When not writing something hot and sexy, TL can be found curled up with a good book, or working on homework with a cute little pixie.

You can signup for her newsletter at:
http://eepurl.com/bvo7fn

# Also by TL Reeve

Saving Their Princess
The Bodyguard and the Dom
Their Secretary
Craving Cameo
All or Nothing
Omega's Heart
Winter Magic
A Wolf's Contract
Private Wolf
A Wolf's Deception
Bear Essentials
Oracle's Vision (with Michele Ryan)
Crouching Lion, Hidden Human
Unrequited Mate